HER

....

Shannon Moose

Contents

Chapter 1

"**K**eep running!"

"I'm trying!" I shouted back.

An ache was making itself home in my chest and it was steadily sharpening itself. Soon enough the ache felt like a knife was carving into me. My chest heaved heavily as I continued to pump my legs. I suddenly realized that running was not the best chance I had and I would have been better off just giving in.

"Cyra, don't give up! Not yet at least!" My brother called once again.

I blinked through the tears that blurred my eyesight as I focused on his form. He was a few paces ahead of me, his scrawny form cutting through the wind with as much difficulty as mine. The only thing that kept him motivated was possibly the fear of a severe beating and the promise of the food in his hands.

I glanced back to see if our pursuers were slowing down. The delta's that ran behind us looked weary, they looked like they were giving up.

A burst of triumph erupted in my chest and I used that to motivate me to run faster.

We took several sharp turns and managed to hide from them. Tucking ourselves in a grove of trees, we climbed high in the tree limbs.

"We did it." I wheezed, clutching the limb for support.

"Yeah, we did." He laughed, leaning back on a large limb.

"C'mon, split the food already then Calix." I hurried.

"Alright, alright." He said.

He dug into the bag and pulled out a loaf of bread and a block of cheese. He split the substances equally and handed me the other half. He took a bite of both and chewed happily before swallowing and continuing the pattern.

I carefully carved a slice of cheese and ripped two hunks of bread before making a sloppy cheese sandwich to nibble on. The food hit my empty stomach, making it groan. I gobbled down the rest of the bread and cheese. I licked my fingers, eager to consume any crumbs that might've escaped my notice.

"We have to go back. . ." He trailed.

"I know," I replied, whispering softly.

"Do you think we'll be punished?"

"I don't know."

He ruffled his auburn hair, a habit he did when he was nervous. His face was blank though, expression was gone from it. A slow breath was sucked through his teeth and he let it out as a sigh before climbing down.

I watched him with slight difficulty. I blinked as my one good eye managed to pick up his form once again. He was halfway to the bottom of the tree.

"Wait up!" I called after and started to clumsily climb down.

He stopped at the base of the tree and waited patiently. His arms were crossed and his head tilted back as he watched me.

"Ah!" I screeched.

My hands slipped and I started to freefall backward. Panic flooded my systems as I fell backward and the air whistled past me. I grunted in surprise as arms came around me and I was looking up at Calix's face.

"Cyra, I think you just broke my arms." He groaned and set me down.

"Well, if that's true then it's because of you being way too scrawny." I poked his shoulder and smiled.

"Ah yes, that is true," He stated, "I mean there is no way you're heavier than me unless you're sneaking food without me."

"As if." I snorted.

Suddenly, a pain flashed through my gut. I doubled over and let out a soft cry. The pain intensified and spread its way through my whole being before vanishing. I looked up to see Calix staring at me in concern.

"It's nothing." I waved him off and stood up.

"We should go back now," He said, "It's almost time for chores."

"Yeah, you're right." I agreed.

We made our way back, slinking through the forest with ease. I felt at home though when we came to the shoreline. A pebble beach stretched as far as the eye could see while waves lapped eagerly like hungry jaws at the shore. The air was heavy with the smell of salt, fish, and other people.

I rushed happily as seagulls cried over a crustacean. The birds scattered at my oncoming presence and I chased after them instinctively. I laughed and stepped into the water, the salt tickling my bare feet and ankles. I looked over to see Calix watching me with amusement.

"Stop acting like a pup, we have a lot of stuff to do." He said after several seconds of eye contact.

I huffed and walked away from the water. The smooth pebbles felt nice on my feet after running over the forest floors. The smoothness of them was like an old memory coming to surface. Nostalgia ran through me as I left the beach behind.

"We could've stayed a few more minutes," I argued.

"No we couldn't," He sighed and shook his head, "Now stop being such an irritating twin."

"I'm the older twin so you should listen to me," I mumbled.

He raised an eyebrow and looked back at me with interest. "What was that?"

"Nothing."

We walked until the house was in view. It stood against the cliff, looking large and menacing. I always thought the house looked like it was ready to swallow any unsuspecting travelers. The windows were large and thin, they were peppered all over the building. It cut from logs giving it a rustic look that should have inspired warm feelings in anyone but to me, it gave off a cold deadness.

I licked my chapped lips and we both headed towards the back entrance. When we came towards the back doors several heads turned towards us. Their faces were gaunt as ours, dull eyes followed us as we slumped against the side of the house.

"Hey look, the disaster twins are back!" A voice sniggered from the dull crowd.

"Hows that eye doing?" Another voice laughed.

I flinched and hid the scarred feature with my hand. I turned my head away and buried it in Calix's side for extra measure. I took a deep whiff of his scent, comforted by the smell of fresh air and leaves.

"Don't pay any attention to them." He said softly.

The jeering eventually stopped. No one had any extra energy to spare, hunger had tightened its grip on them and they settled down. It was silent except for an occasional cough or gurgle of an empty stomach.

Chapter 2

I blinked tiredly as I stumbled my way around the dining room. The bucket of water sloshed in my hands and seemed to get heavier by the second. I slumped to my knees and pulled the rag out of the soapy water. I waited a few seconds, watching the way the water dribbled onto the floor.

The pitter of water droplets hitting the floor was amusing. They stained the wood flooring a shade darker. It made the ground seem like it was dappled with dark stars.

I blinked and yawned tiredly, I sat the rag down on the flooring and started to scrub at the stains. My smock was soaked at the edges and it clung to my knees and legs uncomfortably. I gritted my teeth as my legs became asleep and the numbing sensation sat in. A certain stain refused to come off and I scratched at it with my dull blunt nails.

Little flecks of it started to peel off. I started to scrub at it once again with the rag and was pleased that it had finally come off. I crawled around as I continued to clean the floor.

Footsteps echoed from the hall and a twinge of fear crawled into my throat. I started to furiously scrub at the flooring. A prickling sensation fell upon my back and I realized that I was being watched. I prayed that whoever it was would leave.

A pain curled into my chest, similar to the pain of earlier today. Whoever it was that was watching me had not left. Their strange scent was flooding the room. I flicked my eye to see who it was and was relieved that it was a woman.

She held a confused expression on her face yet power radiated off of her. A mop of platinum blonde hung around her shoulders, several braids ran through the thick tousled hair. Piercing, icy blue eyes were trained on me. They were narrowed in concentration. Her clothes were strange, she wore heavy furs and a cloak made of elk was wrapped around her frame.

She took a step towards me, her footsteps were as silent as a snowflake. Her porcelain skin glowed in the candlelight and she tilted her head.

I swallowed as I noted the height difference between us. She was a towering giant, I could possibly come up to her chest. I flicked my eyes down to the floor in a respectful manner.

She gave a snort. The sound echoed through the cavernous room, bouncing off the walls. She took another step towards me before stopping herself.

"Who are you?" Her voice held a honeyed tone like a serpent. She carried a strange accent as well.

"An Omega." I squeaked and bowed my head lower.

"I did not ask what are you, I asked who are you." She said.

"My name is Cyra."

"I want to see your face."

I slowly turned my head and looked up, swallowing slightly. My face was fully revealed in the light, my hair had been pulled back in a braid so it wouldn't bother me while I did my chores. Now I wished the auburn locks were free to hide my face.

She nodded and bent down, now she was face to face with me. Her cold fingers suddenly seized my jaw roughly. I let out a small cry of pain and fear.

She quickly let go of me. Something unreadable glimmering in her eyes. "What happened to your eye?" She asked.

Before I could reply to her question another person entered the room. This time it was Alpha Greenson. His face betrayed a look of disgust as he eyed me.

"Alpha Lux, is this omega bothering you?" He asked, his fingers twitching.

I went cold as the words came tumbling out of his mouth. Could it be her? Was she the alpha that was so revered? So feared? I touched my jaw, I could still feel her touch. The way her fingers had clenched my jaw.

"No," She spoke slowly, "I was just asking her if she knew when my personal attendant would be assigned."

He chuckled softly. "That certain Omega wouldn't know when the sun rises if it weren't for the sunshine itsel-"

She cut him off. "I don't care what she knows or not. I want to know when I will be assigned my attendant."

He cocked his head in irritation. "If you want one so bad have her."

She turned to look at me and snapped her fingers. "Follow." She spoke.

She whirled out of the room gracefully. I stumbled and scrambled to stand and I trotted after her, eager to escape Greenson's hard stare. Her long legs carried her down the hallways quickly and I had to jog to keep up.

The smock still clung to my body, making it uncomfortable to follow after her. She stopped abruptly and I smacked into her frame. I stumbled back and fell onto the floor.She turned and looked down at me, her expression unreadable.

"I'm so, so, sorry." I stammered, my words shaky as I picked myself up.

"Watch where you're going," She mumbled under her breath, "Your klutzy enough to fall into the sea if you weren't looking."

She opened the ornate door that stood in front of her, walking in with silent footsteps. I followed suit and shut the door gently behind her. Unsure of what to do exactly.

I paused, looking around the room. A large bed was in the center, a thick quilt laid over the mattress and mountains of pillows covered the headboard. The carpet was thick and soft underneath my feet. A window gave a clear view towards the sea. A vanity was against the wall, it's mirror reflecting us in its gaze.

"Now," She said and turned her head towards me, "If you wish to be seen with me, you're going to need a new set of clothes and preferably a bath."

"These are the only clothes I have." I tugged at the smock.

"Then I'll have a new set of clothes arranged for you after your bath." She said and walked into the private bathroom. I heard the sound of water flowing and filling a tub.

"I don't understand." I stammered.

"I'd hardly doubt you would," She said, "Now get in the bath."

Chapter 3

I sighed happily as I laid in the hot bath. Aroma's of flower petals fluttered up to my nose, dulling my senses. I picked up another vial and sniffed it curiously before pouring the scent into the bath. Roses flooded my nostrils and the bath water turned a light pink.

I scratched at my scalp before submerging myself in water. The hot water flooded over my face and I started to wash my hair. The process was painstaking, my hair was knotted and filthy with days of sweat and grime mixed into it. I finally managed to clean it after half an hour. I spent the next minutes scrubbing off the grime that had settled on my skin.

When I was finished, my skin seemed to glow. It was pale and gleaming like the moon, no longer gray looking. I stepped out of the bath and wrapped a plush towel around my body. I relished in the feeling for a few seconds before walking into the room.

Lux was nowhere to be seen. A set of clothes were laid out on the bed though. I shrugged and grabbed the dress, slipping it over my head. I looked down and brushed the wrinkles out and straightened it out. It was a simple cream colored dress that went to my knees. I twirled around happily. A pair of cream flats was by the door.

I put the shoes on and hummed happily. They were a perfect fit. I pondered slightly on how she had gotten the clothes but the door opened and revealed her standing behind it. She still wore her cloak despite the warmth.

"I see you've found the clothes." She eyed me slightly.

"Thank you so much Alpha," I bowed, "I will cherish these forever."

A look of amusement flashed upon her face and her pink lips curled into a smile. Her fingers reached out and held a lock of my hair. Her fingers ran along the lock before letting it go.

"Do your hair, we're to be expected at dinner." She ordered and walked to the vanity.

I ran my fingers through my hair, a slight warm feeling appearing in my chest. I swept my long hair to the side and started to braid it. When I finished, I tied it off using a piece of twine.

Suddenly, Lux reappeared. She had thrown off the cloak to reveal fitting clothing underneath. A tight gray tunic with long sleeves adorned her top and black leather pants were underneath. A pair of thigh high boots were on her feet.

"I do hope you know dinner manners." She said and headed for the door.

I followed after her, silence flooding the halls as we walked. Omega's paused and stared at me, their gazes burning into me. The clatter of dinner could be heard up ahead. The dishes chimed as they knocked together.

I stared in curiosity, the table was filled with important members of the pack and other people who wore clothes similar to Lux. I figured they were members of her pack.

Her fingers curled around my wrist and she pulled me along. I caught a glimpse of interest from one of her pack members as she sat me down beside her. Her hand was still on my wrist even though we had sat down and it stayed there until dinner was served.

The table was quiet. No conversations started up, only stares were exchanged. I could feel Alpha Greensons eyes boring into me. It made me shaky and nervous about what would happen to me after Lux had left.

Finally, a large burly man spoke. He had a bushy black beard that was streaked with gray and he shared the same icy blue eyes that Lux had. "This meal is nice." His voice was thick and it rolled across the room like thunder.

The rest of the table murmured in agreement. Heads bobbed up and down and the table settled in silence. The chiming of knives and forks against the plates filled the room once more.

The man once again spoke, "So Lux, where did you pick her up from?" He made a motion towards me with a large scarred hand.

"I found her scrubbing the dining room floors."

"She belongs on the floor." Someone sniggered.

I swallowed nervously and looked down at my plate. My hands shook nervously and I hid them under the table cloth.

"You know Alpha Lux, most personal attendants simply just stand behind their higher rankings. They don't normally sit at the table with the higher ups. I must say, you are much more relaxed considering your reputation." Greenson spoke.

"Considering my reputation, you should shut your muzzle. I am a guest and should be treated like one." She snarled quietly.

The man who had spoken earlier raised his eyebrows. A wolfish grin was forming on his face. He glanced at me and winked.

"Why don't we discuss the peace treaty between us? I've stated my terms, now yours." Greenson changed the topic.

"A wonderful idea," Lux replied.

The whole room was anxious and she leaned forward. A look of calculations was present on her face. She opened her mouth to speak and the whole table seemed to hang on.

"First of all Greenson, I want a pledge of loyalty from you. You will answer my call if I ever go to war and you will obey my orders. Secondly, I want tributes for the next eight years. Anything valuable you have to offer will be given to me. Thirdly, as a security measure to make that you'll comply with all of these agreements I want several Omega's to come with me, staring with my personal attendant." She said plainly.

I felt my heart stop at her last demand. Fear circulated in my heart as I thought of all the horror stories that circulated around Lux and her pack. The stories were numerous and all were bloody. What would be in store for me?

Chapter 4

I followed Lux back to her room. I was silent through the whole journey back to her room. A twisting pain had filled my heart as I thought of Calix. If he wasn't picked then he would be alone. He had never been alone in his entire existence.

"Pack your bags, come back here as soon as you're done," Lux said as she opened her door. She made a dismissive wave towards me.

I nodded and scurried down the hall. The slippers silenced my footfalls as I walked down the wooden corridor. I slipped past a group of Delta's, they were far too intoxicated to notice me anyways. Opening the back door, I was greeted with the smell of outside. The aroma of the sea washed over me like a wave.

"Cyra!" Calix's arms wrapped around me as he said my name.

"Hey, Calix," I whispered and returned my twins embrace.

"I was so worried, you didn't come back after chore time was done and I was so worried," His speech was rushed as he pulled back and frowned when he saw my apparel, "What's with the clothes? Where did you get them?"

I licked my lips and shuffled my feet. "That's the thing, Calix, I'm leaving," I whispered.

"You're what?"

"I'm leaving Calix. The Weven pack came to visit and their Alpha wants me to come back with her. Greenson has already agreed to it and I'll leave tomorrow." I said quietly.

"No. No, no, you can't leave me!" His arms came crashing around me once more.

"You might be able to come with me. She want's several different Omega's and if she chooses you. . ." I trailed.

He nodded and squeezed me tightly in his grasp. "Don't worry Cyra, I'll figure it out then."

"I have to get my stuff. Then she wants me to go back to her room." I told him.

He let me go and we both walked to the large leaky shack in the back. The door was broken and it swung off its hinges, wide open to the world. That didn't help the smell of sweat, blood, and despair though. Hammocks hung from every rafter and filled the shack from bottom to top. Omega's were piled on top of each other. They slept fitfully and the younger ones were huddled on the floor. They cried and whined for their parents that had abandoned them.

I picked my way through the bodies carefully. In the corner of the shack, the floor was covered in hay. I flopped down the itchy grass and peeled back a floorboard. Underneath was a cloth sack that I had put all my most prized possessions in. I slung the sack on my back and picked my way through the bodies once more.

"Hey, one eye! Where do you think you're going?" Someone sneered.

The whole shack shook as bodies stirred. Everyone was awakened by the voice. They looked around sleepily. Some of them instinctively clutched makeshift weapons in their hands. Everyone knew that when someone slunk into this place late at night, they were usually up to no good.

I ignored the voice and hastened my pace. I could feel arms grasping at me as I carelessly brushed past people. The sack felt like a burden on my back.

"Look! One eye thinks that she can leave!" Another voice joined in the chorus of groans.

I darted out. The night welcomed me in its embrace as I stepped onto the hard packed ground. The shoes protected my feet as I walked along. Twigs that usually sunk into my feet now were deflected off. I looked back to see that Calix had left me.

A stinging pain darted through my chest. I had a feeling that this would be the last time I saw my twin. I tried to shake the feeling off as I walked back into the house. The earlier group of Delta's were passed out drunk on the couch.

I nimbly leaped over the sleeping forms and slid into the hallway. I let out a sigh of relief and started to make my journey back to Lux's room. Luckily, I ran into nobody else.

I knocked on the door. The soft knocks echoed through the hall-way. I cringed at the noise, hoping I hadn't managed to disturb anyone. The door swung open and I was met with her silhouette lounging in the doorway.

"Oh good, I was afraid someone finally killed you." A slight tone of sarcasm slipped into her speech.

I walked into the room and sat the filthy stained sack in the corner of the room. I fidgeted nervously and stood in the corner. A little bit of my hair had slipped out of the braid and was wildly hanging in my face.

She licked her pearly white teeth, her canines glinting in the candle light. She shut the door and slunk to her bed. Her hair was still done with the careless braids tangled through it. She paused, turning to me.

"You never said what happened to your eye."

"You never asked again."

She snorted in amusement and sat on the bed. She patted a spot beside her, motioning for me to sit. Her body language was casual and careless.

I sat beside her stiffly. My heart pounded out of my chest. I couldn't tell if it was from fear though or the warm fluttery feeling in my stomach. Either way, I felt uncomfortable as the feared Alpha leaned close to me. The tip of her nose barely brushed mine.

Her breath was sweet as she spoke. "The fear pouring off your body in waves only makes me want to hunt you down. I would try to control it if I were you."

I shuddered slightly, nodding my head. "Yes, Alpha."

She pulled away. A hunter's smile graced her face. "You're expected to sleep on the floor tonight."

"Yes, Alpha." I murmured.

I slid off the bed and curled onto the plush carpet. Humility stained my features. This was better than sleeping with the other Omega's though and I should count myself lucky. Suddenly, a pillow landed beside me along with a blanket.

I greedily grabbed the items and wrapped myself up in the blanket. I gripped the pillow tightly and made a noise of content. The pillow was large and soft. It was something I never experienced.

"Thank you, Alpha," I whispered quietly.

"I suppose it would have been cruel to make you sleep like that."

Chapter 5

Morning seems to come far too early. I groaned quietly as I was shaken awake. Drool still ran down the corner of my mouth as I sat up, trying to remember my surroundings.

"You should wipe that drool off." Lux's voice pulled me from my stupor.

I jumped and wiped the drool with the back of my hand. I blinked sleepily and stood up shakily. The room seemed in order and Lux stood in the center looking exasperated. Her cloak was slung around on her shoulders once again.

"Finally, I thought you would sleep forever. We need to head out now." She turned and opened the door.

I scrambled up and grabbed the sack. It had sat in the corner, undisturbed by anyone or anything. I opened it though to make sure that its looks weren't deceiving. When I was satisfied with the looks of the contents I trailed after her.

She walked with confidence down the hall. Her tall frame blocked my view of anything that laid ahead but even with my weak sense of smell I knew what awaited us. Her body swayed down the corner and I was left scrambling after.

Just as I had smelled there they were. Seven other Omega's stood at the front door. Their starving frames identical to my own. They bowed their heads respectfully as she sashayed past them. As I scrambled after her, their faces wrinkled in confusion.

I looked at each face. I prayed that among the group there would be a boy with auburn hair and dull blue eyes that matched my own. My heart was wounded though when I saw that he wasn't. He hadn't been picked. We had always known we may lose each other. We had thought only death could separate us but now we were being shown otherwise.

"Cyra!" Lux's voice called from ahead.

"Coming!" I whimpered.

I trotted next to her, my head bowed. Tears leaked from my one good eye. They streamed down my freckled face and blurred my weak vision. A hand reached out to roughly grip my jaw and I recognized her touch instantaneously. Even though her touch inspired fear in my heart, it also put a warmth in there too.

She pulled my head up and I was face to face with her. Some raw emotion lurked in her predatory gaze as she searched my face. Her fingers relinquished their grip on my jaw. They now slinked their way up to my cheek and settled into an almost soft caress.

Her face softened. Her thumb moved to brush a stray tear from my cheekbone. She kept her hands there for several seconds until a voice broke her from the embrace.

"Lux! The boat is awaiting your arrival!" The bearded man from last night was suddenly there.

"Ah, yes sorry about that Ivor." She apologized.

He raised an eyebrow as he glanced in my direction. He seemed curious about why I was still here. He didn't say it aloud though, instead, he turned and walked towards a schooner that awaited us.

"That's my Beta," She said, "He's been with me a long time."

"Oh," I stated.

I glanced behind me to see the other Omega's being rounded up like sheep behind us. Several members of Lux's pack ushered them along. Occasionally they would snap their jaws and the Omega's would cower and run.

I walked up the gangplank uneasily. The boat's floor rocked back and forth underneath my feet. A lulling motion that would have otherwise soothed me if not for my state of emotion now. Instead, it only rubbed salt in my wounded heart. If I went across the sea then I would never see Calix.

Tears threatened to spill once again. Lucky for me the session was ruined by the herd of frightened Omega's. They stumbled around, fear lurking in their eyes and the scent of it was pouring off of them in waves.

A Delta spoke up, "Where should we put them?"

Lux glanced at the crowd in disgust. "Put them in the bowel of the ship." She flicked her fingers at them.

The Delta that had spoke opened up a large hatch that laid in the center of the ship. Another Delta growled and shoved me into the group. We were led down the steps, the inside of the ship smelled of salt and filth. I glanced at Lux's fading figure. She was walking to a cabin, either oblivious or uncaring that I was being put down here.

I grunted in slight pain as I was shoved. I fell on my knees but I caught myself from falling any further. I stood up and brushed off the pain from my stinging palms. My knees were bruised and bleeding.

I sighed and found a corner to sit in. Despite the smell and darkness that flooded the bowel, it was spacious for us. Of course, it was filled with cargo and barrels and they swayed and slid as the boat sailed but it was still better than what we were used to.

"Hey, one eye," Someone called out, "Do you know what's going to happen to us?"

I swallowed. "No."

"Maybe they'll use us as bait for the wild animals." Someone whispered.

"Or they'll murder us and use our bones for decor." Someone said half-heartedly.

A silence set in after that. Horrible fantasies of our fate sprung in everyone's mind. The boat groaned and swayed every second. Footsteps from above were heard and water would occasionally come and trickle down upon us. We were drenched after what felt like an hour but no one knew the time that had gone by.

Abruptly, the hatch swung open and footsteps were heard. We all scattered, hiding in the small cracks and sliding under things. Everyone held their breath as we saw who it was. Lux stood there, her expression haughty and the elk cloak now on one shoulder.

"Cyra, I would recommend you getting your ass out here now." She said calmly, yet as she held up her hand to clean her fingernails they were stained red.

I shook slightly and squeezed out of my hiding place. The barrels shifted and allowed me with ease to clamber out. I stood in front of her, my hands shaking slightly.

"I'm here," I whispered.

Something changed in her suddenly. Her arms reached out and enveloped me, pulling me close to her frame. I was surprised to feel hard muscle underneath her clothes. She hugged me tightly, her cold face pressing into the crook of my neck.

"I didn't know where you were." She mumbled against my skin.

The motion sent chills down my spine unlike any other. They weren't chills of fear, they were something else. I tried to shake off the feeling though as she pulled away.

Chapter 6

I sat in the captain's quarters, my legs tucked up in the hammock along with the rest of my body. I watched lazily as Lux paced back and forth, huffing and puffing before sitting down and continuing the cycle. Her hand had been freshly scrubbed of the blood that had covered it earlier.

I found out that she had beaten the Delta that had mistakenly put me with the other Omega's. The blood had dried in the time it had taken to find me. I sighed and slid back into the large hammock, it swung with the motion of the ship. It was slowly lulling me into sleep.

I yawned and blinked, stretching out before curling back up again. The pain of leaving Calix was still fresh but it didn't hurt as much if I didn't focus on it. I wondered what he was doing now. Dusk had fallen hours ago, now the night reigned with the stars and the moon in the sky.

I peered down at the sack. It had been a long time since I had brought it out and now that it laid only a foot away from me I couldn't help but ache to pull out its contents. I slowly slid my hand down, watching Lux pace the floor. When I finally grabbed the edge of the bag I pulled it up, the fabric ripping.

I watched in horror as my most prized possessions spilled onto the floor. I flipped out of the hammock and desperately grabbed at the trinkets. I swooped them into my arms, holding them close.

"What's this?" Lux questioned, holding a creamy, thick paper that was rolled and tied with a ribbon.

"That's mine!" I flailed my arms in an attempt to get the paper, dropping all my other items.

She looked down at me curiously. Her eyes scanning the other items on the floor. She bent down to pick up a bronze gilded soft hairbrush. She turned the hairbrush over and looked back up at me.

"Did you steal all of this?" She dropped the hairbrush carelessly onto the ground.

"No! These are all mine!" I protested, tears welling up.

"There way to nice to belong to an Omega. Where did you get these?" She asked snidely.

I looked up to see her face full of skepticism and cruelty. I looked back down to see the handheld bronze mirror. I picked it up and rubbed at the ornate C that was carved in the handle. I looked into the reflective surface and saw my imperfect feature.

It was a hideous thing. My left eye had a large, thick scar that went over it. The scar ran from my eyebrow cutting through it, to my cheekbone. My actual eye though was the real ugliness. The milky blue film obscured the whole of the orb. Marking it blind.

Finally, I whispered hoarsely, "My mother gave these to me before she found out I was an Omega. She and my father were the packs Beta's."

Lux's face changed. The cruelty of it melting and being replaced by pity. She bent down and set the paper down. Her hands gently pushing the mirror down so I could no longer view myself.

"I see." She said softly.

I let out a sniffle, the warning of my oncoming tears. I blinked them away though and started to pick up the little bits of jewelry, putting them back into the ripped bag. I paused though when my fingers brushed against a necklace. It was the present she had given me before my ranking ceremony. It was gold with a moonstone centerpiece.

Lux's hand grabbed the necklace and put it into the bag for me. "Why don't you rest?"

I nodded, climbing into the hammock. I didn't feel like resting but I feared to disobey her or voicing my complaints. I turned my back on her though and closed my eyes. I faked the sleeping, my mind racing.

I heard the knock at the door. Lux's footsteps headed towards it and opened it. Another pair of footsteps echoed into the cabin along with her's. I perked my hearing, interested in whoever it may be.

"My Alpha, you wanted to see me?" Ivor's voice spoke.

"Yes," Lux said, "I wanted to discuss something about the Omega I picked up."

"What about her?'

"Something about her, it's strange Ivor. Every time I'm without her it's excruciating. It's like a burning pain in my chest that won't ebb. When I'm near her though, there no pain and I can't seem to function correctly." Her voice was irritated.

"Is that so?" Ivor's voice was smug sounding.

"Is she some type of mystic? I found that she has Beta parentage, could that be why?"

"Lux, it seems that you're experiencing something similar to the mate bond." He said.

"No," Her voice was filled with disgust, "She's a female, I'm a female! Omega's don't have mates!"

"There have been cases of same gendered mates." He said.

"With males Ivor, the only same gender mates have been with males. The gods do not send a mate of the same gender unless they want an alpha lineage to end." She hissed, frustration building in her tone.

"Your lineage won't have to end, you'll be able to have children." He spoke.

"There is no way she can be my mate." She repeated.

"When we get home, ask the mystic."

"I will."

I laid there as Ivor left. I laid there, completely still as Lux blew out the candles and got into bed. I finally sat up as I listened to her breathing fade into a steady rhythm. I waited several minutes for my eye to adjust to the crippling darkness.

I pondered on the conversation I had just overheard. Could it be true? I thought back to the strange feelings I experienced when she touched me. Is that what it felt like?

Chapter 7

The next few days flew by quickly. Lux had talked to me less though, she ignored me often and said I was to stay in the cabin. She brought me my meals and would then leave to go eat with the crew. Today though, she took me outside.

I breathed in the bitter cold air. The wind nipped at my bare skin and whipped my hair back into the breeze. I stared ahead, the landscape ahead filled me with dread.

Snow blanketed the thick pine forest. Grey, bleak mountains broke the tree line, rising in the background like sleeping giants. Even their tips were snow capped, the snow seemed to cover everything. The water around us was icy, thick blocks of ice floated around us. I watched as they bumped off the sides of the ship.

"Come back inside, you'll catch your death out here." Lux's voice called from inside the warm room.

I turned and tottered back inside. The wind had chapped my lips and sent a blue tinge to my fingers. I was grateful to be back inside the cabin. The door shut behind me with a slam, the wind blowing steadily on it.

Lux stood with a change of clothes in her hands. "You'll need these for the journey." She sat them down and paced away.

I slipped on the long brown dress first. The sleeves bunched around my wrists, the dress was obviously made for someone taller. I looked down to see the edges where pooling at my feet. I picked up the next article and pulled it on. It like a furred shorter dress, it fits snugly and the sleeves were billowy. I put on the cap next and slipped on the thick boots.

I looked back to see Lux staring. I flushed, my cheeks turning red. How long had she been watching me? Her eyes trailed along my entire body, her face just as flushed.

Finally, she cleared her throat. "Um, you look nice in that style of clothing." She mumbled.

"Thank you," I bowed my head, "It was generous you provided me with it."

"Don't think anything of it."

She opened the door and motioned for me to follow. I tripped after her, the long underneath dress making it slightly difficult. She stood by the rowboats, climbing into one with the grace of a queen.

I had more difficulty. I stumbled and tripped into the boat, landing promptly on her lap. I blushed once more and scrambled off clumsily. I looked to see Ivor in the boat as well. His face broke out into a smile, he tried to hide it though.

The rowboat lowered into the icy water. Miniature icebergs floated past us, bumping into the sides of the small boat occasionally. I gripped the front of my dress tightly as a splash of freezing water landed on me. The sensation was enough to make my teeth chatter instantly.

Lux glanced at me. Her eyes betrayed her concern for me as she undid the clasp to her cloak. Her swift fingers quickly placed the heavy cloak onto me. She re-clipped the clasp and adjusted it like a mother fretting over a pup.

Ivor raised his eyebrows at the action. His eyes flickering from her to me. "Alpha, would you like my cloak?" He said.

"No.I find the brisk air of our homeland, comforting." She said.

"Where are the others?" I asked.

No other rowboats were depleted. In fact, the ship looked deserted as if everyone had disappeared. Not a living thing stirred on the deck.

"They'll be meeting us at the house," She said, "I asked that they leave later."

I nodded. I peered over the edge of the rowboat, curious of the water. It was an inky black color unlike the navy blue of the sea back home. This water looked hungry as if it would happily swallow us into its dark, freezing depths. I shuddered at the idea and pulled away.

"Do you like water?" Ivor's voice cut through the silence.

"The sea has been my friend for as long as I can remember," I said quietly, "Besides my twin, it's the only constant in my whole life."

"You have a twin?" He inquired.

"Yes, he's back at home though." I fidgeted with the ends of the cloak.

The silence cloaked us after that. Lux had a painful look on her face and she would look at me every few minutes. Ivor was quiet as well, he observed us as he rowed the boat. Soon enough though, the boat hit land.

I lurched forward unsteady on my feet. Lux's arms wrapped around me, keeping me on my feet. Her face scrunched in disgust and she released me. She stepped out of the boat hurried.

"Allow me to assist you." Ivor's large hand enclosed my own as he helped me step off the boat.

"Thank you."

I dug my boots into the strange, foreign terrain. Unlike the pebble beaches and hard packed dirt, I had lived my entire life. The earth here was soft and broke apart easily. I took a step forward and I sunk down a little.

When I around I realized Lux and Ivor were far ahead. Their bodies were slowly being swallowed by the thick pines. I hurried after them, the cloak dragging behind me and the ends of my dress tripping me.

Lux stared at me in annoyance. "Oh my moons," She growled,"We'll take forever to get back with you!"

"I'm sorry!" I stammered.

Her arms reached out and hoisted me up. I screeched in surprise, causing her to stiffen and pause for a few seconds. Then she slowly shimmied me onto her back, my legs wrapped around her hips and my arms enveloping her neck.

"Just hold on, okay?" She hoisted me up once more and started to walk.

She was not bothered by the extra weight and managed to even outpace the giant Ivor was. I began to doubt though that I was any extra weight to her. She carried back prey that was larger than me. I could feel the lean muscles under her back working and I guessed she could probably lift at least twice her weight.

"Enjoying yourself?" She asked.

"Thank you for carrying me," I mumbled in her ear.

"Don't think too much about it." She said.

Chapter 8

"We're almost there," Lux said, sliding me off her back.

I let out a small cry of surprise and stumbled onto my back as I hit the earth. The snow seeped past the layers of clothing, chilling me. I pushed myself back up and brushed the snow off.

"Are you okay?" Ivor asked quietly.

"I'm fine, I just bruised my tailbone," I mumbled, rubbing my lower back.

"Come on, we're losing daylight." Lux's voice cut through.

We nodded and followed her lead, Ivor in front of me while I hung in the back. We marched up a rocky hill with little difficulty for them. I slid and fell through in the middle of the trudge and skinned my hands. The blood trickled down my fingers and left scarlet droplets in the snow.

Lux tutted and glanced at my hands. A flash of concern lurked in her eyes. She hid it though and looked further ahead. The pine forest was just as thick as it was when we had entered it and it looked like it wasn't ending soon.

"Cyra, come here." She ordered softly.

I trotted up to her, my palms still stinging as the blood continued to flow. I tried to tuck them into the billowy sleeves of my dress, hoping to hide them. I knew though that it was futile, she had smelled the blood the minute my skin had opened up.

"Let me see them." Her voice seemed tired yet filled with unease.

I slowly slid my hands out from my sleeves and showed her my palms. The blood was slowly drying yet it continued to pour from my hands. It stained my nails and fingers as it flowed past.

She sighed deeply. Her head shook slowly and emotions swirled over her face. Her long, slender fingers trailed over the minor wounds. She stained her own fingertips and pulled them away from my palms.

"What am I supposed to do with you? I can't even trust you to walk on your own without you hurting yourself!" Her voice turned hard along with her features.

"I'm sorry," I whispered, stumbling over my words.

"Just shut up!" She growled.

I nodded pitifully and started to back away slowly from her. The anger seemed to flow from her in waves, tainting everything around her with fear.

"What are you doing," She snapped, "Didn't I say I can't trust you to walk on your own?"

"Yes." I stammered, shaking.

Suddenly, her arms wrapped around me. Her grip was like iron and she pulled me tight against her chest, squeezing me. The embrace almost seemed like a hug, but I did not return the embrace for fear of upsetting her. She picked me up and swung me onto her hip much like a mother does to a young pup.

"At least this way I can trust you not to get hurt." She huffed.

I trembled slightly, unsure of the sudden change of mood in her. The anger had disappeared and in its wake, the only thing left was her fretful attitude. I glanced around as I hung onto her tightly, fearful for her next mood.

Ivor caught my gaze. He winked at me in a reassuring way, a smile growing on his face and overtaking his features in such a way that it made his large, scruffy beard vanish.

I sighed tiredly and tucked my head against Lux's shoulder. The steady beat of her heart was audible through the marching beat of her feet. Her body seemed to sway much like the waves, lulling me into a defenseless state. I yawned quietly against her tunic, the warmth of my breath causing a puff of smoke to appear in the air.

I closed my heavy lidded eyes and took in a deep breath. I feel into a state on light sleep and enjoyed the half-formed dreams that came to me as I fluttered in and out of consciousness. The dreams made little sense and were jumbled together as if they were a kaleidoscope.

Promptly I was pulled from my state after what felt like thirty minutes. Although, when I looked at the sky I saw it must have been an hour or so instead. Lux put me down, checking my hands for the injury.

"The house is just past these few pine trees," She muttered, "You'll get a bath, bandages, and a new set of clothes."

I nodded silently, lifting my gaze to hers. She seemed so much calmer, tamer in a way. The angry outburst of earlier had almost been lost to my memory.

She pulled away and started towards the direction of the house. Her frame was almost lost in the branches of the pines and the shadows of the night. The only sign of her presence was her lingering scent of jasmine and frost.

I trudged after her, my feet sinking further into the snow with every step. I pondered slightly on how she and Ivor managed to walk on top of the snow. I kept the thought tucked away as I ducked under low hanging branches.

"We're here," Lux said as I caught up with her.

I gasped slightly at the sight in front of us. The house was large compared to the one that I had grown up in. The clearing it sat in was completely taken up by the huge stone structure. Its tall, foreboding frame seemed as if it touched the very sky. Windows were scattered everywhere, allowing the occupants to view the outside easily. The gray stones blended the residence seamlessly against the backdrop of the bluff behind them.

Lux walked up to the giant and flung open the pine doors, she swaggered in with confidence. Her head was lifted high and she reminded me of the first time I had seen her in the dining room. A cheer roared in the house and various people swamped her.

Ivor was next to enter. A look of happiness swelled over him as a woman of his age leaped into his arms and a swarm of children flooded around him. He let out a booming laugh and picked the smaller ones up, hugging them tightly before letting them go.

I hung back, unnerved by the number of people. They all were quite large like Ivor and Lux. All of them had the tall, lean frames. Some of the faces were marred by scars or markings, making them look cruel. I let a whine of fear slip past my lips involuntarily.

Heads began to swivel in my direction. Curiosity and disdain painted on their face. Whispers swirled into the air and replaced the cheerful noise.

I took a step back, feeling small. My breaths came quickly as a mind-numbing fear sat in my bones as people poured from the house, surrounding me slowly. I skittered back and backed into a tree, hitting my head hard.

I felt a small trickle of blood crawl down the back of my neck. The scent of the metallic substance spread quickly in the cold air. They drew in closer at the scent and some let out animalistic growls.

I cried abruptly, tears leaking out of my eye. The trees' needles poked my back and urged me to climb. I was afraid to turn my back though yet the need was stronger. I swiveled around and scampered up the tree as if my life depended on it.

I clung tightly to the trunk of the tree as I went higher than I planned. I felt the pine shudder as someone pulled on the branches below, climbing after me. I started to cry harder, the tears freezing on my face. I was aware of the pain in my palms, they had reopened during the climb.

"Cyra!" Lux's voice suddenly called out.

Everything went still. The shuddering of the branches quit and I knew that everyone had frozen at the sound of their Alpha's voice.

"Cyra! Cyra, get down!" She ordered.

"No!" I stammered.

"I will give you to the count of three. If you aren't down by then. . ." She threatened.

I started to scramble down, ignoring my better judgment. The bark sliced and cut my palms worse as I haphazardly scrambled down. I stood shakily on my feet as I jumped to the ground. The people from earlier were behind Lux now, they peered at me.

"Come on," She whispered, "It's going to be okay."

I fearfully clung to her side, staining her clothes with my bloody palms once more. My heart continued to beat its way out of my chest, threatening to leap out of my throat. My grip tightened as she turned to the crowd, taking me with her.

"No one is to terrorize this girl, is that understood?" She asked, her voice holding an edge to it.

"Yes, Alpha." They murmured.

"Follow me." She said gently to me, walking through the crowd.

Hello! Sorry for the slight break, I had some family things pop up. Anyways, thank you so much for reading and don't forget to vote, and comment! :)

Chapter 9

"Are you okay?" Her voice brought me out of my panic as she pulled me into a large, lavishly decorated bedroom.

"Yes." I squeaked.

Her eyes shined and she wrapped me in an embrace. Her face pressed against the warmth of my neck, chilling me. She took in a deep breath, slowly letting me go.

"I'm sorry for my strange behavior. I don't know where it comes from." She mumbled.

"It's okay Alpha." I dipped my head.

"Please, just call me Lux." She said.

"Okay, Lux."

A silence flooded the room. She looked down at the floor before getting up and disappearing behind a door, leaving me. I sighed and looked around, noting the sumptuous qualities.

A large, ornate four poster bed was at the head of the room. It was made of dark wood and the mattress looked soft and inviting. A thick, luxurious fur blanket laid on top and a mound of pillows crowned the whole thing. I sunk further into the thick, maroon carpet as I took a step.

Various tapestries hung around the room, each one depicting some story. A family tree hung over the fireplace at the side of the room. The flame inside of the stone hearth, looking cheery. It illuminated the family tree and the names attached to each branch. I glanced to the other side of the room to see a wardrobe and a vanity, each one adorned with carvings.

I caught sight of myself in the vanities mirror and sighed. My hair was straggly and my dress was stained. I licked my chapped lips and they cracked, a thin stream of blood erupting from the corner.

I walked to the door Lux had disappeared behind and sat in front of it. The wood was so thick that it made it impossible for me to hear beyond it. I waited patiently for her to reappear and give me instructions or a purpose.

I laid my head on my knees and closed my eyes. Darkness flooded me and I sighed, clutching the carpet. The softness of it tickled my fingers and I didn't worry about staining it anymore. I thought briefly about Calix. I wondered what he was doing, was he missing me? Was he okay? Did the other Omega's treat him better now I was gone?

Lux suddenly opened the door, pulling me from my thoughts. She had changed into a pair of new clothes, her hair wet and dripping on the floor. I watched the droplets hit the carpet, dappling with a darker color.

"Hey, there's a hot bath waiting for you. I'll get you some new clothes while you're in there." She said.

"Thank you." I dipped my head in appreciation and slipped past her.

I shut the door gently and glanced at the steaming water. The tub was a large one, the porcelain sides gleaming in the light. I struggled out of the layers of clothing, dipping my feet into the bath when I was done with the dreaded articles of garb.

The water rose in clouds, warming my icy skin. I sunk into the warmth eagerly, the water swallowing me whole. I looked around the rim of the tub, various bottles of liquids were perched. I picked one up and poured a little of the golden brown substance into my hand before lathering it in my hair. The scent of honey and vanilla wafted past my nose as I scrubbed the scent into my locks.

I opened another vial and scrubbed the contents onto my skin. The scent of brown sugar overcame me. I took a deep breath and enjoyed the mingling of smells. My stomach growled after several seconds, reminding me I hadn't eaten. I scrambled out of the bath and found a towel.

I wrapped the towel around my frame and slipped out of the room, looking around. The carpet felt twice as plush on my bare feet compared to earlier. I clutched the towel tightly and walked out, wondering where Lux had slunk off too.

"Lux?" I croaked.

The door opened and I jumped, the towel slipping slightly. I flushed as Lux stood in the doorway a nightgown hanging over her arm while she held two plates of food. Her eyes wandered over my frame, looking at me with slight hunger.

"Sorry!" She said hurriedly and closed the wide open door behind her.

"It's fine." I stammered.

"Um, here I brought you some clothes." She sat the plates down on the bed and handed me the attire.

"Thank you." I grabbed the gown and walked back into the bathroom, feeling her eyes on me the entire time.

I slipped the embroidered gown over my head. Little blue birds were sewn into the gray fabric, they carried little flowers in their beaks. I admired the nightwear before trying to adjust it. It hung low, showing off my jutting collarbones. I sighed and opened the door, padding out.

"I'm glad it fits you." She mumbled and leaned back against the pillows.

"Thank you." I stood there nervously.

"Come, sit down and eat." She offered, patting a spot beside her.

I nodded and crawled into the plush bed. I wanted to roll all over the softness of the mattress but held the desire in. I picked up a plate and waited for her to start eating, the respectful thing to do when dining with an Alpha.

She didn't notice and instead stared at me. "Why aren't you eating?"

"I'm waiting for you to start."

She raised an eyebrow and picked up a plate. She grabbed at a roll and sunk her visibly sharp teeth into the bread item. She chewed slowly and watched me with anticipation.

I picked up the turkey leg and sunk my dull teeth into the meat. I groaned in appreciation as the flavors exploded in my mouth. I eagerly devoured the leg, licking my lips when I was done. I moved my way to the next item on the plate and happily finished the whole dish.

She watched with surprise. She gave a small chuckle and took the platter from my hands, setting it down beside her.

"You eat quickly." She noted.

"I don't get a lot of food back home," I said.

"This is your home now," She sat up and placed a hand on my shoulder, "You'll get as much food as your stomach can handle."

I smiled faintly at the idea. "I'd like that."

Hi! Don't forget to vote and comment! Sorry about no music I couldn't find a fitting song for this chapter but if you have any ideas for one don't be afraid to comment it! :)

Chapter 10

"Lux?" I whispered.

"Hmm?" She groaned in the dimness of the room.

"I'm sorry, were you sleeping?"

"It's fine, what is it though?"

"Where would you like me to sleep?" I asked.

A pause circled through the air, stalling time itself. I waited anxiously for the answer, my body tired and worn from the long journey and terror infusing meeting with her pack. I waited patiently though.

"You could sleep with me. . ." She said softly, the offer hanging in midair.

"With you?" I repeated.

She nodded, her outline faint in the flickering of candlelight. "You can if you want to." Her voice held a hopeful lit to it.

A prickle of fear coursed through me. The offer was a dangerous one, something that Alpha's gave out when their boredom and frustration gave in. If I accepted her offer though, what would that mean for me? Would I be given a life of luxury before being tossed aside for a newer Omega? Did she really mean just sleep or was she thinking of what I was thinking?

"Can I be excused to take a walk Alpha?" I squeaked, my hands shaking visibly.

"I told you to call me Lux." She frowned and leaned close.

"So sorry Lux." I shuffled back.

"You can take a walk, be sure Ivor is with you." She jerked back suddenly, a look of hurt and annoyance on her face.

"Thank you." I skittered off the bed towards the door.

I took a deep breath, sliding against the door as I stepped into the hallway. I tucked my knees against my chest and looked around. I had no clue were Ivor might be and I had no desire to disturb him. Standing back up, I decided to wander the hallways. I hoped to meet a friendly face, preferably one of the Omega's from my pack.

The floors were made of stone as well as the walls, giving the whole corridor a freezing atmosphere.Various other doors were lined on the sides, some of them empty while others had occupants. I jumped as one door opened, revealing the woman who Ivor had been holding.

I froze, waiting for her to notice me or brush past me like others did. Now that I was up close to her though I noticed her features. She was definitely older than Lux. Her hair was done in a braid, silver streaks peeking through brown. Her features though were slightly marred, three parallel scars slashing across her face. I could tell though that she was still good looking.

Her owl like eyes flickered over me, a flash of recognition going through them. She smiled, unlike most smiles I had seen this one reached her golden eyes. She took a step forwards.

"Hello, Cyra." Her voice was strong yet pleasant.

"Hello." I stuttered, ducking my head nervously.

"There's no need to be nervous, perhaps you don't know me? I'm Saskia, Ivor's mate." She chattered, hooking her arm through mine.

"I saw you earlier, were all the children yours?" I asked, letting her lead me down the hall.

"Yes they were, we have six of the little rascals. In fact, I'm going out to find them, would you care to join me?"

"Sure, I've never really been around kids though," I said nervously.

"What? That's impossible, you mean you've never had the joy of being around the munchkins?" She exclaimed.

"No, the pack doesn't let the pups associate with us," I replied.

"Oh. . ." She trailed.

We walked in silence after that. Our footsteps silenced by the uproar that reverberated through the walls. The floor turned from stone to pine wood as we walked into a large den. Couches and chairs were draped in fur and covered with people. Various social rankings lounged around, happily chatting. A few pups sat on the floor playing with their toys.

A few heads turned towards us, then went back to their talk. We walked through the throng of people, some of their eyes narrowing in confusion as they saw me. The talk around us died down into suspicious whispering.

"Um, Saskia I don't think I should be here," I whispered, tugging away.

"What? That's nonsense! Here, could you hold Tulip for me?" She turned around to reveal a small girl in her arms. She handed the pup to me before walking a few feet away.

I stood there awkwardly, holding the little pup in my arms. I glanced down and gave her an uneasy smile. She flashed a grin back, revealing her tiny sharp teeth. I shifted her weight in my arms. She couldn't have been more than a year old yet she made me more nervous than the full grown wolves around me.

She gurgled, reaching for my hair. Her chubby fist clutched the fiery locks and tugged on them. I grunted slightly in pain and looked back down at her, my nose wrinkled. She gurgled again and let go of my hair, patting my nose.

"Thank you so much for holding her."

Saskia suddenly appeared again. She was holding three more children, these ones being even younger than Tulip. Two more hung around her hip, looking around the ages of five and seven. I blinked when I realized they were all boys.

"I can hold her on the way back." I offered.

"Really? Thank you so much!" She squealed happily.

"It's no problem," I assured.

I picked my way through the crowd and let out a relieved sigh as my feet hit the cool stone flooring of the hallway. I readjusted Tulip in my arm and watched in amazement as Saskia walked through with grace and agility despite the cooing triplets in her arms and the two children clinging tight to her.

"Do you remember the way?" She asked, slipping past me.

"No," I mumbled, slightly ashamed of my terrible sense of direction.

"It's okay, this place can be a maze sometimes." She said cheerily.

I followed after her, my footsteps loud and clumsy compared to hers. I was beginning to wonder if the silent footsteps were something they were born with instead of learned. It seemed even the children knew how to mask the sounds of their footsteps.

I skittered to a stop as she halted suddenly, without my realization we had made it back to our starting point. She opened the door walked in, glancing back at me.

"Are you coming?"

"Yes," I said.

Chapter 11

The inside was surprisingly spacious. Tulip continued to clutch onto me tightly, her little claws digging into the fabric of the nightgown. Saskia huffed in disdain as she nudges away a small pile of thick, dogged eared books with her foot. "Ivor! Your books are all over the floor!"

A grunt from another door that was across the room alerted us where the hulking man was. A few thudding footsteps sounded and he made his appearance. A smile flitted across his face as he saw me and he bowed slightly.

Tulip scrambled down from my arms and towards Ivor. Her footsteps were shaky and unsure as she toddles towards her father. Her older brothers easily beat her, the triplets were only several footsteps in front of her despite her best effort.

"Ah, it's nice to see you settled in and cleaned up Cyra!" Ivor cried happily, picking up the children in a huge bundle.

I nodded and stepped back nervously, he held the scent of something strange and old on his clothing and it unnerved me greatly. The children and his mate paid no mind to the scent and carried on with their lives, Saskia hummed and plucked one of the triplets from his arms and carried him off into another room.

"Where is Lux? Did she go out without taking you with her?" He pondered aloud, setting the rest of the children down for them to go and play.

"No," I stammered, "She went to bed and permitted me to go out for a walk."

"Alone?"

"No, I was supposed to find you but then I got caught up in something," I said my voice still wobbling as I jerked my head towards the children.

"Perhaps you should go back to your room then, you have a big day tomorrow after all." He smiled and his large paw guided me out the door and into the hallway, facing Lux's room.

"Ah, okay." I nodded and trod towards the door, lifting my knuckles to knock.

Before my fist made contact the door already swung open, revealing Lux towering over me with mixed facial expressions. Her eyes narrowed as they closed on me and she gave a curt nod towards Ivor. He returned the nod and went into his room, leaving me alone with Lux.

"You took quite a long walk." She said slowly, opening the door for me to walk in.

"I didn't take a walk, I helped Saskia find her children." I trilled.

She closed the door and nodded slowly. She took a deep breath and slid her eyes back towards me. "I thought about my earlier proposition and realized how that may have sounded and I had a pallet prepared for you." She flicked her wrist towards the pile of blankets that laid on the floor.

"Thank you," I said and slunk around her, not trusting the way she held her body tight.

"It was no problem." She walked back to her bed and pulled the furs over her.

I arranged the blankets and fur accordingly for me to lay on, relishing in the softness of the fur I had chosen to lay on. It was like the hide of a deer but thicker and more gray and dark brown in color, elk hide. I pulled a woolen blanket over me and laid my head on top of several other garments.

Despite the prospect of sleeping on the floor, it was far comfier than any other arrangement I had been in. I pulled the blanket closer to my face, enjoying the slight comfort it brought me. I rolled over as I felt eyes boring into my back. I was correct because as I turned my head I could see Lux's eyes glowing, the flickering of the candles around us making them look ominous and hungry.

I clutched the blankets tighter and stared down respectfully. Her gaze continued to linger before she rolled back over suddenly. A sigh erupting from her chest as she did so. Her hand reached out and she snuffed the life out of the candle beside her, plunging the room into complete and utter darkness.

"Goodnight little Omega." She said softly, her tone almost tender.

"Goodnight," I replied, my tone soft.

I didn't sleep right away though, I forced my breath to even out so it would seem like I was. My eyes were wide, watching her form to see if she would fall for the trick. My breath flitted past the furred blankets, making the little hairs sway in response to my breath. My body was impossibly still for a sleeping person but she wasn't looking at me so that didn't matter I figured. I shifted in the pile of furs and blankets so they accommodate my tiny, scrawny frame better. I was slightly fearful of suffocating under all of the weight.

She seemed to have fallen for the little trick because she didn't say anything else. I could hear her light breathing fading out as she seemed to fall deeper into her sleep. She rolled, turning to face me. She seemed peaceful, more mellow. I could almost mistake her for friendly almost. She was hardly friendly, her constant mood swings put me on edge. Would she embrace me or yell at me for my incompetence? I was having difficulty picking out the patterns of her behavior.

I closed my eyes, thinking of Calix. I missed his warmth, the way his scrawny arms wrapped around to protect me from anyone who would slink into the Omega room to pluck out the prettier ones for a night. Was he curled up in the corner missing me? I thought he would be, all alone without anyone to talk to for the night. I was missing our late night talks, the whispers we'd share as we talked about what we saw that day. If he was here, what would I tell him? The strange behavior of the higher ranking wolves towards me? The stiff, hungry look Lux flashed every so often? I pulled the coverings around me tighter at the remembrance, swallowing. God's, help me. I prayed silently as I closed my eyes to sleep.

Chapter 12

Last nights sleep could be described fitful at best, constantly tossing and turning. I would awake from half formed dreams, blearily checking my surroundings. Some times thinking I was back on the ship, then back home, I would always come back to the realization though that I was here. In this cold, barren land with Lux.

When morning came she was the first to wake, she threw a bundle of clothes at me, demanding I get up. I clumsily climbed from my nest of furs and began to dress myself when she slipped out the door. My fingers fiddled with the long, tunic like dress and the furred over coat that went along with it. I was pleased to find the leather boots fit though and I trotted out the door to see Lux awaiting me.

"We're going to see the mystic, best behavior." She warned, wagging a finger towards me.

"Yes Lux," I mumbled quietly.

She nodded, seeming pleased with my obedience and started to walk. Long legs and swift steps saunters in front of me in a statement that was obvious that she was Alpha, that she was in charge. It was such a difference to my own awkward strut.

My head swirled with the idea of meeting the mystic, excitement and fear. Every pack had one born every fifty years or so, strange children born of no status but could commune with the god's themselves. What was this one like? Were they harsh and cold? Old and feeble like the one back home?

I was so caught up in my thinking that I almost did not notice that we we're outside nor that Lux had stopped in front of me. I walked into her and whined, rubbing my forehead. She was all hard muscle under those pretty features, how a true Alpha should be.

"Watch yourself," Lux said slowly, turning her head to glance back at me. "One of these days you'll run into someone who'll take offense."

"I'm sorry," I bowed my head, my eye flicking up to glance at her. "I wasn't watching where I was going."

"That much is obvious."

She turned back around, flicking her wrist as a motion for me to hurry to her side. I trotted up, my feet dragging in the thick snow that was a seemingly constant blanket around the area. I glanced to see her feet were perfectly balanced, walking with ease over the snow. It must be something their born with, I decided.

We came to cabin, the cedar logs relatively fresh and new on the outside. A fire burned, the gray smoke trailing from the chimney lazily. I took a deep breath in, my weak nose detecting strange spices and someone else beyond the door. I couldn't tell anything else but I knew Lux could, her senses were much more alive then mine.

"Best behavior," She warned once more, her voice even colder than the ice and snow around us.

I nodded frantically, my locks bouncing along with my head. I stared down at my palms and clenched my hand, the pain stung. They were still raw, no longer bleeding through. I perked though when Lux swung open the door and stepped in, a blast of heat escaping to embrace me. I hurried after, looking around the strange room.

The walks were scribbled over in chalk drawings, strange runes and symbols. Silks and heavy blankets draped everywhere along with hides made me feel as if I were in a cave of warmth and softness. As my nose had detected, plants of every sort and type hung drying. Perhaps it wasn't always snowing here then. I reached to touch one, a bundle of flowers that were once a violent red but were reduce to the color of drying blood.

"That's poppy," A new voice spoke, feminine and young.

I turned to look and found myself staring into two mismatched orbs, one sky blue the other a deep brown. They were painted in traditional makeup, swirling lines of gray, black, and blue. The colors of this particular pack. The eyes blinked and I noticed it belong to a face and body. It was a girl, a few years younger then me. Hair the color of wheat and skin like cream, she was dainty yet carried herself with as much pride as Lux.

"Welcome," Red lips parted to speak and the girl smiled. It was an odd smile though as if it knew more than she let on.

"What's wrong with her? With me?" Lux stressed, stalking around the various pieces of furniture with various things covering them.

I studied them, the crackling of the fire was filling my ears as I zoned out. Books littered the tables and chairs, old and thick with dust. They contained writing I couldn't understand, smudges against my eyesight. Bowls of bronze filled with offerings of crystals, herbs, spices, and bones to the gods in the corner at an altar. Little clay statues of them all representing them.

"Lux, why so harsh to her? Can you not tell?" The girl spoke, waving an arm to me. Brackets jingled and I noticed the makeup went down her face, past her collar bones and disappearing in her folds of clothes.

"Tell what?" Lux spoke, her voice even and calm although the way her jaw tensed spoke she felt otherwise.

"If I say it, you'll fly into a rage and deny it." The girl spoke with her mouth curling into a smile. She obviously knew she was right about this issue, the smug look on her face spoke that in volumes.

Lux's eyes sparkled with anger and her jaw tensed even further. "She is not." She said slowly, her knuckles tightening.

"Shall I consult the gods? Should I, conjure up the god Ukaya, ask his advice on whether or not I'm right?" The girl said and plucked several things from several altar bowls as she spoke, tossing them into a larger copper pot.

Lux said nothing but gave a curt nod. She did want her to consult the gods. A tricky task for anyone but a mystic.

The woman smiled, the same smug smile that a person who knew they were right would wear. She picked a bone and sat it in the pot. I peered in curiously, seeing all the salts, herbs, and various other ingredients. She pushed my face away and plucked a hair from my head then Lux's. She wrapped it around the bone in a neat little bow, then took a log from the fire and set the items in the pot on fire.

I jumped back as the flames lurched up hungrily, lapping at the items in a desperate attempt to burn more, burn longer. Their greediness was the end of them though and they died quickly. The mystic plucked the charred bone and presented it to Lux, smirking.

Where the hair had been tied was a etched in heart, burnt into the whiteness of the bone. It was obvious, no mistake could be made about the shape nor what it could represent.

"Will my line end?" Lux spoke, her voice low and grave sounding.

"No," The mystic replied, "It will flourish."

Chapter 13

It's been exactly five days since we saw the mystic.

As soon as Lux had her answer, she whirled and stalked out of the snug little room, saying she was going hunting. She'd left so quickly, so suddenly that she didn't bother to shut the door to the little hut and a wind full of snow blew into the soft, warm area. She stalked off to the woods from what I could see, what little vision I could use to see with anyways.

With that, I'd been left behind with the stranger who ushered me out, saying she was busy. She said that if I was up to it that I should follow Lux. Though she said it in such a way as if she knew I wouldn't be able too.

She was right.

I couldn't follow nor track Lux in the weather and was so unfamiliar with the woods that I trotted back to the lodge full of wolves. Now with the free sudden free time I planned to find the other Omega's, the ones that had came here with me and the ones who had been in the hold of the ship. Though as soon as I stepped foot into the lodge, I found myself bombarded with strangers and their scent, the dizzyingly long corridors, and the firm knowledge I could not find them by myself all likely. So I promptly found a nice spot to sit, in the area that Saskia had taken me to find her children in.

I sat there all day and night, hopefully for a sign of Ivan or anyone else that I might know. I was sorely disappointed when no one showed up. Just strangers with strange accents, clothes, and all around no familiarity. I quickly found myself missing my brother more than ever, Calix would have never left nor abandoned me. A funny little thought considering that I was the one to abandon him in a way.

So for the remainder of the days I spent my time exploring the area. All around the house my petite little frame made its way through the area. Poking and searching through the area curiously. I made myself familiar with the halls and the rooms, searching for the other Omega's I could not find. My weak sense of smell and bad vision didn't help much. Though I found that as long as I kept my head tilted up, I could smell things quite faintly.

Throughout my little exposition of the lodge, I found a few places of interest. One was a rather plush and warm nursery. The scent of newly born wolves was something my nose could easily detect. When I first entered, my ears were bombarded with the wails and cries of little infants and several women who bustled from one area to the next, tending to them with a calm demeanor. I learned that the lower placing wolves sent their young children here till they were off duty.

It was a nice place, the women were kind and one had spotted me and had me help. Though as the day went on, the nursery emptied and I was scooted along as my help was no longer needed.

The second place was the kitchen. Pastries, meats, and food of every kind imaginable was found. Older children ran amongst, snatching pastries and eliciting playful curses and the shooing along of them as the workers quickly rushed to replace whatever item that had been taken. Some mistook my tiny frame for that of a childs and pushed a few pastries into my arms, saying that I needed to gain my strength for the pack. I had quickly thanked them and went to stuff my face, never having received food such as this before. I found that blueberry turnovers with powdered sugar was my favorite.

The third and somewhat most intriguing area that I had found was by complete accident. I had been so completely and utterly immersed by a strange scent that I had caught wind of, I had not realized I had stumbled into an area that I had never been in before. By the smell, no one else had been either. Though one strange and entirely familiar scent clung to the air and so heavily saturated the air that I could not lose it. It was then that I stumbled and fell against a wall. Though the wall was suddenly not there as I went to catch myself and then one of the stones I had put my hand on sunk in and the wall swung open.

I had to pick myself up, brushing myself off. I looked in confusion as I saw sunlight and a lush scene of greenery I had seen nowhere else in this cold frozen land. I was so enamored with the sight of the ferns, flowers, the whole lot of it all. It was as if someone had taken a cut of the jungle and placed it in the middle of the frozen wasteland. I look down to the floor, curious as to see green grass even. I stood and brushed myself off, looking back to see the wall was back in place and a shot of panic flooded through me. There had to be another way out. So I stood and followed the odd scent once again, wandering around aimlessly.

Exotic flowers as dainty as lace and in colors I could not even imagine dotted the landscape as while as lush ferns, beautiful grasses, and everything in between. I found myself overly hot and I discarded the boots, the overcoat, and stripped down to the linen shift I had put on first. I was almost completely bare but finally comfortable as I wandered. Eventually, I found what had drawn me to the area in a set of two twin pools with water as clear as glass. Tiny, tropical fish with silver tails and flashing tails in every color of the rainbow swam in them. It had been the water I smelled.

I sat besides one of the pools, almost forgetting my panic as I stared into the water with the little fish. I dipped my hand curiously into the water, trying to clumsily catch a fish but my reflexes were so slow I could not. I furrowed my brows, sitting back. I looked around, seeing reflective glass panels. It struck me that I was in a very large greenhouse somehow. I sat back, trying to quell my nerves. I was worried about being caught by someone, it struck me that I wasn't supposed to be in such a lovely place. I certainly didn't belong here, a place of beauty and I seemed to be the one imperfection.

Suddenly, I heard it.

"You," The voice was one that I still shuddered at hearing, "How the fuck did you get in here?"

Chapter 14

I could not help but be slow to turn and face the speaker. I was filled with a thick knot of dread that grew and twisted in my gut and rose to my lungs. Twisting blooms of anxieties and thorns of fear crawled and made their home in the cavity of my chest like some sort of strange flora that had the aims of killing me. Sweat prickled the back of my neck despite having cooled off from the lack of clothing and the pile of it besides me. I finally managed to gain the strength to do so though, slowly turning my head to see what amounted to the sight of a butcher covered in the blood of his latest slaughter.

A somewhat strangled scream escaped past my lips and I flung myself backwards in some sort of instinctive feel to protect myself. Hands, feet, any limb immediately went to work of back pedaling in a quick, hurried manner in order to get away from the blood soaked stranger. It was as if my limbs had been replaced by sandbags as I struggled to stand or pull myself up, well aware that crawling backwards was not an efficient way of escaping. The metallic, coppery scent of blood filled my nose and vaguely, I wondered if my guard had been so far down or if my sense of smell lacked so greatly that I could not smell the death and blood that wafted off of the individual.

He was a tall, towering man as I had noticed most of the men here tended to be. I suppose that the jokes and jests of the packs of further north being a hardy stalk wasn't just jokes. He might've been labeled as handsome if it weren't for the sneer and disgust that twisted his pale face. His cobalt eyes narrowed and the butcher started walking forwards. His heavy, fur lined clothes dribbled with a little blood and stained the grass with scarlet droplets. Sandy blonde hair that grew in waves even had the liquid staining the edges. He looked like something from a story told to scare young pups.

"I didn't see you with the others, how the hell did you escape?" He asked, seeming more pissed and confused than anything else. He kept walking forwards, seeming to have every confidence that I wouldn't manage to either escape or maybe that I would accept the clarity of my fastly approaching fate.

I felt I could do neither.

Finally, with what seemed like a herculean effort, my limbs twisted and my body forced itself up off the ground. I was screaming again without realizing and I darted forwards with the fleet footedness of an Alpha it felt like. I'd never felt like I had ran so fast nor took off so quickly in my life but I realized with some weighted down dread that I had no idea how to escape this place and so I was doomed to play cat and mouse until the cat caught me. I could feel myself shake as I kept at it, my limbs desperately pumping in an effort to put and keep distance between me and the stranger.

I didn't see you with the others.

The thought flickered across my mind, the others. The other Omega's. I immediately knew what had happened to them, the sudden clarity of the moment had broken across my mind as to why this pack never had Omega's. It made a whole new sense of guilt, dread, and fear grow wild in my already thumping chest. The feelings were so thick, I thought I might trip and fall dead from the lack of oxygen that was pulled into my lungs. I kept scrambling, tears leaking from my one good eye. It took me a few seconds to realize I was crying as I hadn't noticed till my vision blurred and the screams that tore from my throat were still hoarse.

I knew I couldn't run forever, that it was a matter of time. Still, disappointment and bitterness filled my chest as I felt rough hands that easily overlapped my frail wrists jerk me back. I screamed again, head whirling around to face the other. My other hand immediately went to try and claw with blunted, unhealthily chipped nails at his fingers. I could not die, not yet, not here.

"Let go! Let go of me!" I wailed like a miserable child, never had I made such a fuss in my entire life. I tried to dig harder, inflicted no damage besides a few little red lines but that was hardly enough to earn me freedom. "Let go!" I snarled and begged, tears clotting my vision.

"Shut up!" The strangled snarled, revealing canines large enough to rival even Lux's. His fingers curled around the thin bones harder, causing me to drop in a strangled whimper as I felt bones shift and crackle. "Your kind is a weakness, a disease to this pack. The only thing you're good for is sacrifices to the gods. Accept your fate and maybe I won't bother to have a little fun and I'll make this nice and easy for someone like you." He threatened and something dark lurked behind those eyes, dark enough to make my blood run cold at both threats and the thing that lurked behind those eyes.

"Samael!"

A familiar voice broke through, a voice that I was sure that had to have been sent from the gods. I craned my neck despite the uncomfortable position to see Lux, a rather angry Lux. Her hands clenched tightly at her sides, her body taunt with the intensity of it. It was the kind of anger that reeked of Alpha. Enough that it made me cower as I felt the waves roll off of her figure.

The man who was holding me immediately dropped me like a bag of flour. "Lux," He said cooly, looking over to the Alpha. "I was just cleaning up the last of them. What're you doing here?" He looked rather stoic in the moment as if he had been about to read a book and then had been interrupted. As if he hadn't been about to murder someone in cold blood.

"She's not to be touched Samael, she's a personal pet." Lux continued, walking over to the both of us. She reached down and as if I was a pup, swooped me up and placed me against her chest. Her arms secured firmly around me as she clutched me close. "You should clean up, running around like you are puts a bad name on the family." She said smoothly, stepping back.

I lifted my head up, clutching onto Lux for dear life. Part of me was frightened, shaking still. I was convinced that if I were sat down even for a second, that the other would immediately snatch me up into his hungry jaws and I would be lost. The idea of what had happened to the others rang through me clearly, the blood on his hands had stained parts of my own skin and clothes. I couldn't help but stare down to the stains, half listening to their conversation. Family, was the other related to Lux? A small part of me didn't want to know, didn't want to ask.

"Of course Alpha, I'll get cleaned up right away." The tone in his voice suggested he heavily hated being told what to do. It was one of sarcasm and uncaring. He stepped back, lifting up his arms as he studied the blood covered fabric. "I suppose you'll have me throw these away too? Anything else in my life you want to dictate?" He said rather snappishly, rolling his eyes.

"Sama-"

"You know what," He cut her off, lifting up a hand. "I don't really care. I know the answer." He shook his head and turned, stalking off.

I watched, watched like how prey watched predator to know when it's safe to go. I watched his form disappear until I was sure it was safe and it was the last I saw. I watched even when Lux started walking, trying to rub my back tenderly and ignoring the shakes and involuntary flinches. The idea of what had happened, the concept still ringing clear in my mind.

One way or another, I was going to meet my end here.

Ahaha remember when I said to update regularly? Well... Let's just say life threw me an extremely sucky curve ball but now I'm back! I'm hoping and I mean really hoping to be back permanently! Thanks for sticking around so long!

Chapter 15

I was silent the entire trip back to the room, Lux leading me like a little pup along the halls as we traveled. I was still silent, I hadn't spoken a word and she hadn't bothered to say anything. My wrist was badly bruised, more than likely sprained or fractured. My mind was an endless torrent, swirling with the news and revelations of what had just happened. All the tribute Omegas were dead. Lux was related to that monster.

She pulled me into her room or was it our room? She'd never given me my own, she had told me that I was staying with her. I held my arm for a moment, looking down at the various bloody stains on my shift that Samael had left when he'd grabbed me. The coppery scent had never left my nostrils and the newfound knowledge of whose blood it was only made my skin crawl with disgust. I needed a bath and a way to erase everything that had been revealed from my memory. For once, I felt a bitter pang of relief that Calix hadn't been chosen, that he'd been spared from such a fate that the others faced.

"I'm. . . I'm sorry about what you saw." Lux said awkwardly, finally breaking the silence between us as she stood there.

I simply lifted my gaze to her, jaw set and somewhat emotionless as I took time to calculate a response of some sort, unable to form words. Finally, my mind grappled around something. "What I saw? Do you mean what I've realized? What goes on?" I said, my voice surprising even me in its calmness and I wonder if it's because Lux hasn't shown me what a danger she truly is yet.

"It's not what it seems."

"Really? Are you really going with that? You. . . You slaughtered them. You left them as bloody offerings to whatever monstrous gods you worship and you tell me that it isn't what it seems?" I whispered quietly, the horror evident in my features as I finally whispered aloud the knowledge that I possessed.

Lux went silent, her face like stone as she stared at me. She no longer looked or acted apologetic, just... Stared. "Maybe it's best you go bathe and go to bed. It's been a long day." She said, her voice obviously stating there was no choice in the matter and it was an obligation.

I simply set my jaw, and looked away. I didn't dare refuse but my blood boiled for a moment at being told what to do. I put it away though and made my way to the bathroom, drawing the hot water and slipped out of the bloodied clothes and into the water, letting it hold me in its own watery embrace as I closed my eyes, trying to push down my feelings as I tried desperately to connect what was exactly going on. Why was this happening? Why sacrifice Omegas? Sure, they weren't too overly useful but did that really equal death in this harsh snowy wasteland? The room too brought questions to mind, how idyllic and peaceful it had seemed yet it held horrors unimagined still.

When the bath went cold and I could no longer sink into the freezing water, I stood and dried myself, the fiery locks of auburn had curled round my head like an unmanageable, frizzy halo. I brushed it back with fingers pushing through tangled locks and wrapped the towel around myself. I hadn't bothered to grab a nightgown or any sort of slip so I crept into the room. Lux was asleep or perhaps faking, I wasn't sure. The room was dark and silent, her body covered in furs as her back faces me, rising steadily. A small pile of clothes had been gathered in the few days, my own sets of fabric. I clumsily grabbed till I felt the thinner fabric of a sleep slip and pulled it over my head, allowing the towel to drop. Of course, my pallet was thankfully still intact. Lux didn't want me sleeping with her despite the connection we seemed to share according to the mystic.

I crept towards the well made pallet and crawled onto of thick furs, peeling back the top layer in order to lay down. My head hit the pillow but unlike previous nights, I couldn't fall asleep. I thought of Samael, Calix, Lux. The Omegaless pack and the children within it that hadn't found their rank. I thought of a thousand different ways to escape and a thousand and one ways that I could die in each scenario that I conjured in my mind. It was hopeless, it was my last chance. It was everything and nothing that I could do. I would simply die here and no one would know of my fate. I would be sacrificed like a pig or elk, my throat slit, and if I was lucky, my thighs clean from blood.

I didn't sleep at all, I couldn't sleep at all. My eyes ached, I was sure they had bags underneath. The morning sun was rising, dawn pushing her sunlit fingers through the windows and breaking through the dark of night. I fluttered them close as I heard Lux stir in her sleep. To my knowledge she typically rose around dawn and let me sleep for several more hours before waking me. I assumed that it would be the same routine. Occasionally I'd wake to catch Lux changing or in some form of getting ready and I'd quickly shut my eyes and act as if it hadn't happened like I hadn't caught sight of her midriff or the elegant curve of her neck as she pulled her hair up or braided it in the strange northern style. So I assumed she would rise and get ready and leave me be. She had no reason to really interact with me all of a sudden.

So I listened to the quiet steps of her morning routine and it felt like ages with my back turned her and how I had to pretend asleep. I secretly thought she knew I was wide awake. After all, it was hard to fool an Alpha. Though it seemed she didn't notice or didn't necessarily care. I heard quiet steps approach me, I tried my best not to stiffen. This wasn't part of the typical routine I had spent time memorizing in my days here. Then suddenly, I felt a pair of soft lips brush against the skin of my cheek, grazing it in a sort of chaste kiss that made my heart thump a little harder than it should have.

"I'm sorry Cyra." Her voice cut through the mornings air, soft and gentle, murmuring against my skin and I felt the heat radiate from her body. Then suddenly, it was gone as I presumed she drew back and I heard footsteps retreat and the closing of the door. Signaling the routine was complete and the Alpha was gone.

Chapter 16

I spent my time in the morning alone, bundled in the furs of the pallet. It was always freezing whenever morning came and especially when night descended. It was strange to think that it was only fall with the extreme temperature. Fall at home had been mild, a few chilly days but it scarcely felt as cold as this unless it was the dead of winter and even then it was far milder. So I waited for Lux to come and rouse me as she typically did.

She never came though.

Realizing that the Alpha was going to avoid me, I roused myself up. I ditched the sleeping slip and pulled on the far thicker one and the overdress that was still a little too big for me. Pushing my too small foot into the oversized wool socks and then into the fur trimmed boots, I was almost ready to go and tend to my usual duties that I had found. I was free to go and do whatever I assumed, I hadn't ever been told otherwise and so I went and busied myself with kitchen chores and the nursery area.

I pulled the uncontrollable mane of hair into another braid, difficulty assuming since my hair was wet when I fell asleep and it was as tangled as a briar patch. I gave up after a few tries, hair sticking out and pieces pulled out to frame my face. I pointed ignored my reflection in the mirror as I most often did and stepped out of the safety of the room and was met with such a commotion, it made me falter in my steps.

Wolves rushed back and forth, busy with armfuls of items and wearing clothing that looked nicer then usual. Furs that weren't so matted, a woman had ornaments weaves into her hair, the gold pieces glinting in the lights of the home. It was such a jarring sight compared to the usual warrior gruffness that the women and men here shared. My mind scrambled for some sort of explanation of what was going on.

Saskia appeared arms carrying the small daughter who was dressed for the occasion as well, the small girl wearing a rather ornate gown trimmed with white hare fur. Even she was wearing something as equally ornate, hair decorated with glinting ribbons of gold as well. "Oh, Cyra!" She hummed brightly, her good eye gleaming in excitement. It was obvious she hadn't discovered my earlier disappearance or my newfound knowledge. Maybe she didn't even know.

"What's going on?" I asked, eyes flicking around to study the new details. "Is it some sort of holiday?" I asked, wondering if it was the creation day of one of their gods.

"It's the day of legacien." She simply replied, smile still bright and the excitement of the pack now obvious. "Didn't Lux tell you? She went to go look for you and help get you ready yesterday." She said, shifting the gurgling child onto her hip. "Do you need help? No offense dear but. . . You are expected to wear something a little nicer." She said carefully.

I felt stupid for a moment, inwardly groaning. Legacien day was a sacred holiday to all packs. All the days differed but they all celebrated the same thing more or less, the creation of the packs that our gods had released onto earth. Today it seemed, I would come face to face with whatever monsters that the northerners worshipped as their creation gods.

"No. . . She didn't have the time." I answered, it was the true after all. I didn't necessarily want to talk about the Alpha much less talk to anyone that resided here. Yet. . . I couldn't help but feel the she-wolf's innocence or perhaps naivety to the whole thing. Perhaps she truly didn't know? Maybe it was a secret that the Alpha and her family kept to themselves. I desperately wanted to believe that. I laughed, shaking my head a little as I held my arm for a moment. "I understand. The help would be nice. I'm not sure what I should wear." I admitted somewhat lamely.

Saskia clicked her tongue and gave me a warm smile. "Don't worry, I understand. Your position is. . . Unique." She said oddly, "I'll take you to the Mystic, she'll have you properly outfitted."

At the mention of the Mystic, my mind came back to the bone and the small etching that had been carved into it. Saskia's oddness the way she had said position. I pushed the thoughts that arouse with it away, there wasn't any possibility. None whatsoever. It was me being hopeful, wanting to improve my status, me being greedy for being more than a useless Omega.

I allowed Saskia to lead me outside to the hut the mystic resided in, memories of odd body paint and warmth flooded my mind as we stood outside the door. I could already smell the faint hints of the odd spices and herbs as Saskia knocked, awaiting the arrival of the godly woman.

A moment later, her pale face appeared. All curling red lips pulled into a smile, the same dark colored paint swirled onto her face and I couldn't help but wonder if it was permanent rather then painstakingly applied everyday. She motioned us in, the jingling of bracelets calling us forward as we stepped into the hut. It was the same as before, items haphazardly scattered, silks and velvets aligning the area like a nest.

"I'm supposing you've brought her to be properly outfitted?" The mystic mused, looking towards the Beta female. We had thankfully left Tulip back at the house, I could only imagine the trouble the toddler would get into here.

"Yes mystic." Saskia mumbled, dipping her head. "I thought it'd be best if you were the one to prepare her for tonight."

"Very well, now be on your way. Thank you." The girl replied with a bow of her head and watched as the Beta female left with a sigh.

"Honesty, is Lux so stubborn? After communing with the gods and all? Does Ukaya's words mean nothing?" The girl scoffed, hands thrown in frustration and the bracelets jingled more madly. "It doesn't matter, she has, I mean has to allow you to accompany her tonight. It wouldn't be proper otherwise." She said and shook her head. "Now, have you bathed today? Surely you don't plan to go like that with your hair? You know what? Nevermind, you get no choice in the matter." She scoffed.

"What's wrong with m-" I was about to ask with a frown before she promptly shushed me.

She gripped onto my arm, pulling me through the mess of the hut. "No time to speak! I must get you ready to meet the gods, Erisim will be most interested I'm sure. You must be bathed and dressed accordingly as well. No more common clothes, strutting around as if you aren't Lux's mate." She clicked her tongue.

"Mate?" My heart clenched, the thought I had been carrying, the painful way my body contracted upon her arrival, the sudden ferocity and gentleness Lux treated me with. "Omegas don't have mates, we don't even procreate!" I argued.

"Is that what you've been told?" She clicked her tongue, leading me to a room with a bath, much simpler then Lux's as she ran the water. It looked cold. "You have so much more potential then that. Do you think Lux would have made it with some Beta male? Do you not see her temper? She could never carry a child anyways!" She scoffed, "The pack would have to change hands to. . . to." She faltered for a moment, picking up strange bottles filled with petals and oils, dumping them into the tub. She shook her head. "No, no, we need you. Now, get in the bath."

I looked at her with hesitance, processing the information that the mystic had just bestowed upon me. I had a somewhat good idea who she faltered of mentioning. Samael. My blood ran cold at the idea of him ruling a pack, governing it towards bloodshed. At the mention of the bath, I regarded it was suspicion, staring down at it.

"Well? Hurry! We don't have all day!"

I clumsily and hurriedly undressed, stepping into the water. Just as I had thought, it was as freezing as the landscape outside. Hands came on my shoulders and promptly pushed me into the tub, I shuddered and yelped at the sudden exposure. I had been pushed down to my shoulders, body quaking and suddenly another bottle of oil was poured over my head, making me gasp for a moment. The strong smell of something floral, a flower I couldn't identify overcame my senses.

"We have a lot of work to do it seems."

Chapter 17

Hours had passed by since I had been dunked into the practical ice bath and smothered with various floral oils and perfumes. If I hadn't known any better, I would have said I spent days in the mystics hut, letting her tend and fit me as she saw fit. When I had first stepped from the bath and was enveloped in a warm towel and sat besides the fire, I had been ecstatic. The warmth of the crackling flames had filled my body fast enough and the process that ensued afterwards had almost made me feel special. Almost as if I truly were important.

The mystic had rubbed me down with various oils, leaving my pale skin soft and glistening in the firelight, the scent vaguely reaching my nostrils as the delicate balance was enough to alert others it was there but not enough to over power them such as the bath had been. The various oils had left me smelling new as if I had reborn, soft sweet smells and a clean crisp as if she had somehow managed to capture the scent of fresh snow and mixed it in with what I had found to be the scent of snowdrops and hellebores. Then she'd began the long, time consuming task of opening various chests, dragging out luxurious clothes one could only dream to even touch.

Long, furred dresses made of mink and a cowl lined with the fur of a snow white hare. Then she'd dropped them back into the chest and brought out even more elaborate and wonderfully designed outfits till she seemed to have settled on one. Holding it up against me, I almost wanted to step back, afraid of somehow spoiling such a grand gown. It was something a Luna would wear, beautifully trimmed and hemmed to show off the body yet no plunging necklines nor skin tight areas to create an oversexed appeal. I came to hold it against my chest, fingers lightly running over the front of it, amazed still.

"Well? Go on, put it on already." The mystic urged, already opening more chests for gods know what.

I couldn't possibly refuse the offer, it was absolutely gorgeous. So, dropping the towel I held around me for this entire time, I immediately went to the task of putting it on as carefully as possibly as if to avoid any damage to the gown. It was impossibly luxurious, truly. Floor length and styled in the similar way as the shifts I wore, loose enough to not show curves yet tight enough to avoid the situation of looking like a billowing tent. Elegantly long, drooping sleeves came down to my wrists, tiny crystals painstakingly sewn along to create the effect of glittering snow along them as well as the rest of the dress. The neck was cut into a halter, comfortably coming around me as the white fabric glittered beautifully.

As I touched the fabric for a moment, the mystic came and gently brushed my hands back, placing a golden girdle around my waist, giving me the sudden appearance of a little curve as if to show I had a proper middle after all. It was a simple golden belt, I glanced to see her placing a gorgeous cloak lined with the fur of what might've been a white fox at some point or another, the cloak embroidered with golden thread woven into patterns as well. A pair of dainty yet hardy looking boots were set aside as well as several other things.

"Come now, I have to do your hair. I can't believe you tried getting away with going like that. You looked like you just rolled out of bed." The mystic complained, guiding me to sit by the fire as she took an iron rod, placing it besides the heat in order to warm as she brushed my hair gently and scented it with perfume. "Honestly, what would anyone do without me?" She scoffed.

Picking up the rod by the cool end, she began to wrap the tendrils of deep red hair around, carefully unwinding to reveal a luscious curl. She began to repeat the process over and over.

"I had just rolled out of bed and I thought I looked decent enough for just waking up. Besides, I fell asleep with my hair wet." I couldn't help but defend myself as she curled my locks, waiting in between time to warm the rod and then repeat the steps.

"Of course you thought so. No one ever wants to admit they look like shit." She grumbled under her breath, finishing up with her work.

I went quiet, slightly put off and pouty at the insult. I simply set my jaw and crossed my arm for a moment, waiting for her to finish up. "Well I didn't want to put any effort into something that I'm not even going to be apart of. Lux isn't going to let me stick around very long." I argued back finally, my voice sulky.

"Don't worry, she'll let you. She has too, it's not even an option." She argued back for a moment. "It's a celebration of the gods and Lux may think she can take the wild seas and crush mountains under her feet, she can't change the will of the gods." She said.

"There, now your done." She said, stepping back. She pulled and fluffed out the curls, finished with her work apparently. "Just a little more and then you'll be free to go. It's about time for the big celebration anyways."

I watched as she took out a little wand with bristles on the end, sticking it in a mix of black ooze. Upon being instructed to look up, she did so and winced as she felt the other applying it to her lashes though when she was done, they looked far more dramatic and darker.

"Now then, we're done." She said, grabbing the cloak and clasping it over my shoulders. She adjusted the hood carefully and helped put my feet into the boots that had been set aside as well. "I'll escort you out to the ceremonial grounds and then Lux will have to see who you are now." She mused.

I furrowed my brows for a moment. "I'm not sure she'll believe you. I. . . I don't even believe you." I admitted as I looked towards her. "It has to be a fluke."

"Then it doesn't explain why she saved you from Samael, her attitude towards you, the fact you're still alive." She mused, taking my hand in her own. "Trust in me, trust in the gods. They don't make flukes as you call them."

With that, she pulled me from my spot and out the door we went. "Head up Luna, look proud." She whispered to me, hand squeezing my own as my foot stepped out into the snowy landscape.

"I'm not a Luna."

"No, not yet you aren't but I know you'll get there. I've seen it."

Chapter 18

The crisp winters blanket had fallen once more over the ground as we moved along. I was convinced it did nothing but snow since I hadn't seen the blue sky once in the weeks of staying here. The sky always seemed to be filled with downy little flakes drifting down or the dark ominous roll of blackened clouds. Perhaps that was just the color of the sky here though, a thundering gray that had permanently made an overcast stain.

The mystic had been leading me for over twenty minutes, deep into the pine wood. Thankfully and yet surprisingly, the dress she'd given me as well as the cloak and boots kept me warm and dry. Though my fingers were somewhat cold, I just tucked them into the little pockets sewn in the inside of the cloak and they were warm and the cold momentarily forgotten about for a few moments till I had to steady myself and take them out. I'd almost hit my head on several tree branches as we walked along so a quickly darted hand in front of my face was necessarily needed relatively often. There was a little path that we walked on but it seemed as ancient as the gods themselves, windy and narrow, clearly abandoned and forgotten it seemed. The branches draped over and a few well sized rocks had lodged themselves into the middle of the hard earth packed trail.

It wasn't long till I heard voices and the faint, drifting smell of a fire came to my nose. I could see shapes, flickering to and fro between the pine needles and the shrubbery that was caked in icy layering as if nature herself had dawned her finery for the occasion. I glanced over to the wheat haired mystic, hoping for an explanation if not a sort of introductory perhaps even a run down of what I was supposed to do as we neared what could easily be identified as a oval shaped clearing.

Instead, she gave me a slightly impatient look. "Well? Go on." She nudged me forward. "You'll find Lux easy enough and I have other things to do to prepare. I've taken you this far."

I spluttered, "What? I can't... I can't just wander in. I'm not even supposed to be here." I whispered, my eyes widening for a minute as realization sunk in. Everyone was going to stare and it was certain that everyone would know who I was once they smelled me. Lux would find me and I'd most likely would be booted from the ceremony and left to find my own way back to the lodge without anyone to guide me.

The woman gave a huff, mumbling something under her breath and she gave me another nudge this time it was harder. I stumbled again, this time at the edge of the clearing. I flushed for a moment, some had taken noticed, glancing towards me and mumbling to themselves before going on with their conversations.

I went to glare at the mystic, swiveling my head back but only found nothing but empty space. She had already slipped away. I set my jaw, I'd have to talk to her later if she bothered to show at all for the festival.

More and more people were beginning to take notice. The earlier ripples of groups had alerted others and my appearance was easy to pick out in the crowd. Everyone was dressed elaborately compared to what they normally wore but I was dressed even more elaborately so compared to them. I stuck out like a sore thumb even still in the pack despite almost looking similar to them.

"Cyra?"

I turned my head once more, recognizing the voice. I'd know that voice anywhere and something stirred in my chest as it always did when I heard it. I swallowed, prepared for Lux to kick me out. For her to stare me down. My mind though fluttered to the kiss on my cheek that had been planted on my face earlier, the warmth that fluttered through me. I wondered for a brief moment if it was true. What their Gods has decreed, what the mystic for spoke of.

She was wearing something completely opposite of my outfit, we almost mirrored each other in fact. It was the first detail I noticed as her tall, strong frame cut through the easily parting crowd. While the warrior women who wore pants and furs had exchanged their gear for more slim fitting dresses or furred tops, Lux had traded her gear for an even more elaborate outfit.

Instead of the typical side elk fur trimmed cape that was typically worn, she wore a golden threaded cape, the fabric dark as coal, trimmed with the glossy black fur of a bear. Her hair was pulled back and looked freshly washed, the elaborate braids she wore now had golden rings darting through her platinum hair. A plain white cloth tunic was worn underneath that and a dark leather chest plate over that. Matching leather braces on her wrists adorned her arms and her pants were tucked into a pair of knee length boots that matched the leather as well.

She strode forward, gently grabbing at my hands with furrowed brows. "Cyra? What're you doing here?" She questioned, eyes flickering over me for a moment, her expression unreadable. "Where did you get this?" Her fingers gripped at the sleeve of my dress.

"The mystic." I simply replied, tugging back my arm. The memory of my discovery was still fresh in my mind despite everything at the moment. I wasn't so willing and ready to forget.

"She ga-" She was speaking when suddenly Saskia showed. All smiles and grins.

"Oh! You look beautiful." Saskia said, smiling as she almost went to touch me and hesitated as if worrying about messing up the outfit. She settled for delicately touching a curl instead. "Look at you," she breathed, "It's like your a proper Luna."

Lux cut back in, jaw set. "Exactly. She does and she isn't." She said, all softness and confusion of earlier dispelled by Saskia's approach. "It's not right nor proper. She's dressed like she's actually someone." Her nose curled and yet despite her harsh words, the action just didn't look... Natural on her features. It looked forced. "She shouldn't be here."

My throat tightened for a moment, biting my cheek. She was right. I shouldn't be here. I should be at the lodge, sulking in a room as I wondered where everyone was. I turned my head for a moment, refusing to let her see how she twisted my emotions like taffy. It was so hard, she was so cold or strangely warm. It was like she couldn't make up her mind. It was like she was two different people at times. Holding me at one time and then pushing me away.

"Then you should've left me back home." I said, glancing towards her as I narrowed my eye. "You should've taken someone else. Not me." I said, brows furrowed with anger. I took a step forwards. "You should've left me with my brother."

Her face changed, morphing as she looked down towards me. Her eyes narrowed for a moment. "It doesn't matter what I should do, what matters is what I choose. I chose you and I'll choose what happens to you." She snapped. Out of the corner of my eye, I could see Saskia backing away. People were staring. Her hand came and gripped mine, her fingers were like iron, firm and strong.

"And I choose where you get to go. What ceremonies you attend, not the mystic and certainly not the gods!" Her voice raised.

And that's when it happened.

Chapter 19

The wind had started to pick up, icy claws of snow and particles of ice drifting about. Gently at first, it started as a soft breeze that had came through as Lux spoke. Then it began to rapidly grow in strength. Whipping around angrily as the inky darkness of the sky snarled like a cornered wolf with teeth bared towards the enemy. It was as if the tempest had sprung from nowhere all of a sudden. The crowded scene the Alpha and I were making by raising our voices had suddenly backed away, their collected mumbles sounding confused and worried. Children were clutched tight to their mothers chest and mates had pressed their other halves to their chests in a protective manner. It was only Lux and I, standing in the middle of it while the storm grew. The blonde had ceased her tirade by then as the wind had grown more fearsome, a solemn look on her face as her jaw tightened.

I on the other hand had wrapped my arms around myself in order to keep the wind from blowing me away. The air felt alive with energy. A crackling steadily filling my ears, something inside me twisted in an uncomfortable manner. I couldn't quite pinpoint what it was but I knew that someone or rather something was angry. My attention turn back to Lux who seemed just as defiant as beforehand as the wind cut around us, encircling us in a flurry and blocking everyone else from our sight.

My mind swirled, thinking of various possibilities. Of gods and the mystics warnings. I clutched to my cloak tighter, the wind threatening to tear it off of my frame. I felt flattened as if the vortex around us was going to rip me off the earth and fling me into the sky. I opened my mouth to speak but the icy air pushed into my mouth and into my lungs, stealing any words that might've been uttered.

Faintly, I could hear Lux cry something out. It sounded garbled as the wind picked up the words and sent them away and I couldn't understand what she said and I was having a hard time shutting my own mouth and even just breathing. Despite the swirling air around us, it whirled so fast I couldn't seem to suck it in before it swept past us. I finally decided to try and crouch down, I felt as flimsy as a paper doll while I forced my body to move downwards. A gust caught me off guard and I sprawled downwards on the the ground, fingers that had been previously clean now digging into the earth as the wind dragged me along like a hungry beast. I let out a cry with whatever air left in my lungs, afraid that I really would be carried away.

I squeezed my eyes shut and that's when I felt familiar hands on my wrist and a presence near me. Suddenly I was pulled up into a sitting position and pressed against a chest. I struggled to open my eyes, already knowing that Lux had sunk to her knees to grab me. I could feel her fingers digging into my back, holding me to her chest as she surrounded me, cradling me from the storm. I felt so small and limp as I buried into her, shaking as the bitter cold surrounded us.

Despite it all, I felt grateful in the moment. Being dragged from home, the horrific discovery, and yet I still felt safe in her arms. Some small part of me was frustrated with myself, angry for my weakness. Angry that in the moment I couldn't find a single drop of hard-heartedness to address her with. I simply pressed my face into her shoulder, ignore the tough leather breastplate she wore, burrowing myself in as I clung to her like a newborn does to their mother.

She only clutched me closer in response, her face pressed to the top of my head and I could feel her lips moving against my curls, mumbling something. Her grip was like iron, clinging onto me as if she was afraid the wind might drag me from her.

Finally, throughout the mumbling I caught what she was saying, repeating over and over. It came in small snatchea, the howling wind occupying my hearing still. The words were being lifted up to the air in as some sort of offering, a plea.

"Erisim forgive me, forgive me. I understand what I need to do just forgive me." She mumbled fervently.

Suddenly, the wind stopped.

I could still hear it howling around us yet the sensation of it blowing was nonexistent. It was as if everything had suddenly faded to a dull roar and all that was left was the blood rushing in my ears. The earlier sensation of discomfort appeared stronger and my body felt paralyzed. I could feel Lux shifting, her face pulling away and looking up. I gathered myself, fingers curling into her clothing as my gaze lifted up.

"You're quite insulting when you refuse to acknowledge what's been handed to you." A rumbling voice spoke.

In front of me was a rather large, godlike man. He was seemed to fill the entire space with his presence, an even gaze falling onto us. His appearance seemed to reflect the packs itself, the same warrior like clothing, the intricate braiding, the only difference was that he was gleaming from head to toe. It was as light streamed from every crevice and pore of his body. His eyes were unnatural as well and I couldn't quite place why those sky blues were so unnerving till I realized that he had no pupils. It was just blue iris, taking up the expanse of where the pupil should be. The blue dots were surrounded by the whites of his eyes almost concealing the unusual character flaw. If gods had flaws that was.

"Consider me insulted for handing it to me." Lux muttered under her breath, soft enough that I almost hadn't heard it.

"You're insulted? Insulted that I insured this packs survival? Insulted at how I've woven the threads of destiny at which your connected to?" The gods voice boomed. "Insulted that I, Erisim have come personally to set the grievance in which you seem so set on creating, straight?"

The wind seemed to pick up again, violently once more. I squeezed Lux for a moment, still unable to find my voice as I took in the fact that a god, a god, had come down before us. I could only hope he wasn't fickle and that Lux would find herself backtracking to her apology.

Lux seemed to realize, her grip on me tightened once more. "No my god." She said, head bowed. It was quite possibly the only time I had seen the other become so submissive and quite possibly the only time I ever would. "I just. . . Don't understand. I don't understand how this is suppose to help the pack flourish. How she's supposed to be of any use, why Ukaya has given her to me."

"Of course you don't understand, not everything is drawn out so simply like the battle tactics you create Lux. Trust in us, in your fates. Something is coming Lux, something dark and dangerous. Trust in your gods, in yourself, and especially in the little one from the southern seas." His head dipped towards me. "She is the key to it all. She'll provide for you and this pack in more ways than just a womb."

With that, the winds began to cease and it seemed so did the god. Unraveling like a ball of yarn, the vortex suddenly ceased and the god disappeared, leaving only us together and clutching onto each other. The remaining pack members having fled it seemed or taken shelter further in the woods. The clearing was empty and she turned to me.

"What are you?" She whispered, brushing back my wind blown hair for a moment.

I wasn't sure how to answer her. It seemed Erisim thought I was more then what appeared. Some part of me, deep down, believed him. "Your mate apparently." I replied.

Chapter 20

We didn't stay for long after Erisim's appearance. We distangled ourselves and I brushed off the fine clothing I'd been wearing, disheartened and guilty about the water and mud stains that had been smeared all over the dress and cloak. I could only imagine the mystics reaction when I'd come back to return the outfit. Though, Lux didn't look any better with wind tangled hair and the mud on her own clothes. It somewhat made my own mess a little less shocking.

Walking back to the lodge in the complete silence of each other's company was maddening. It coated the air with a thick, smothering fog as we picked our way back. Lux hadn't said a word in return to me after telling her what everyone else had been repeating in hushed whispers. A look of silent indignation on her face it seemed as she made her way through the snow with me trailing after here. I managed to somewhat keep up with her, having to trot besides her on the path which lead me to believe it was the reasoning why she was walking in the snow. The path wasn't exactly big enough for us to walk side by side and she kept catching me whenever I stumbled.

When we finally arrived at the lodge, the warmth that leaked from it calling towards me and my snow soaked clothes. I gripped at the door handle, hurriedly kicking at the side of the lodge to remove most of the packed on snow that had found itself stuck to my boots. I tugged on the door, opening it as a blast of heat washed over me. Lux waited for me to walk inside first and I silently undressed myself, removed the cloak from my shoulders and the boots from my feet. It suddenly overcame me how much time the mystic had wasted on me. It had been hours of preparations only to last for less than fifteen minutes.

It was then that I noticed that Lux was trying to talk to me. "Well? Are you?" She asked, pressing on as she looked towards me, her face neutral. She still hadn't seemed to take to the news very well.

"Am I what? I didn't hear you." I responded.

She set her jaw for a moment, annoyed. "Are you going to go take a bath?" She repeated once more, arms crossed. "Or do I get to take one first?"

I paused, "I'm taking a bath." I grumbled and carrying my items, made my way up to our room. Though it was really more of her room, I simply slept in it. I could feel her presence behind me, following me. I choose to ignore it.

Setting my things down, I found the little pile that was slowly accumulating to a chests worth amount of clothing. Thumbing through it, I found a winter shift that I often slept in and went to bathe.

Lux had of course followed me into the room, something sulky and unreadable in her expression as I shut the door.

The bath was quick, lukewarm water that made my cold skin shiver and my hair drip wet and then I was done. The chilly presence of the winter air and the damp condition I was in didn't seem to help her. As soon as I was out, Lux was brushing past me into the room and shutting the door. I sneezed for a moment, sniffling. It was freezing and as I turned to crawl into my pallet of furs and blankets, discovered it missing. A deep rooted sense of irritation filled me. I was miserable, wet, and cold and she had done something with the very little items I could call mine.

I clenched my fists and decided for the time being, I'd sit in her bed. Crawling up onto the large mattress, the soft feather down it was presumably stuffed with slightly sank under my small weight. I seized the blankets and furs, wrapping myself tightly into a cocoon as I shifted my way towards the end, the glow of the hearth warming my face at least as it was now the only thing visible. I sniffed again, the chill that had settled in my bones hard to get rid of. I closed my eyes, Lux wouldn't be pleased. I'd smell up her bed. She'd probably quite possibly would kick me to the floor but at the moment, I was pleasantly warm and somewhat pleasantly pleased at the smell of the blankets. How they smelled of sharp pine and ice like Lux. It was frustrating how she seemed to ease me sometimes, how easily I let myself forget.

It was then at that moment I realized the bed was dipping again and someone had gotten on it. I panicked for a moment but before

I could get up or turn around, my mind registered a pair of arms around me and a chest to my back. I squeezed my eyes shut, mind flooding with several bitter memories. Hands squeezing wrists too hard, heavy breathing in my ear, the trickle of blood that ran rampant down my thighs and the thick scent of an Alpha as they bore down on me. It was enough to cause me to lock up, freeze as I always did and I hated myself even more for it.

"You're going to fall off the bed like that." Luxe voice finally broke through. "You should sit in the middle, not at the edge. You'll fall into the fire with your luck." She spoke, chest suddenly leaving my backside and her arms disappearing as well. I struggled to swallow the bitterness of bile that had risen in the back of my throat.

"I took your furs and blankets to be cleaned. It's been a few weeks so I figured it was time they'd get cleaned." She said, shifting around on the bed as if unsure of what she was doing.

I flicked my gaze back from her and then down. I knew it meant I'd be sleeping here for tonight. It made my guts twist in anxiety yet I bit it back down. I expected for the event to take place. Alphas felt entitled after all, Lux knowledge of me being her mate would only make her feel she had further claim to my body. I fiddled with the blanket between my fingers, looking back up to her. She looked softer now, her hair was down for once, thick and wavy in some areas as it fell around her shoulders. She wore a shirt and a pair of shorts, her skin unbothered by the cold wasn't even prickled.

"Are you hungry?" She asked and suddenly it reminded me of my first night here. "I know you must be. You're always jumping at the opportunity." She said, it sounded like she was vaguely trying to joke. Maybe she was. It was back to this again, back to the warmer side of Lux. The gentle side.

"I could eat something." I decided to respond. No need to make the entire night miserable. I laid my head against my own shoulder. "Do you want me to go get something for us?" Now that I knew my way around, I was sure that she'd want me to fetch things. Maybe I could avoid things if I played my cards right.

"No, I'll get it." She said, getting up. "I. . . I should do things for you I guess. If what Erisim said is true. . ." she trailed again. "I'll be back." And with that, slipped out of the room to leave me to wait.

Chapter 21

W hen Lux came back, we ate in silence and I sat closer towards the hearth. My hair was drying in a tangled mess, the locks curling and waving in a uncontrollable frizz thanks to the added heat of the fire. I was simply glad that I didn't have to sleep with wet hair, I tended to get sick. She took the plates and cups and left before coming back, I gripped at the bed covers when she did. I knew what was coming next, she was a creature of habit after all. I'd studied her routine and knew she would crawl into bed and settle for the night. I wouldn't have anything else to do but comply with the ritual and turn in for the night as well.

Just as I expected, she crawled underneath the blankets and furs, her back facing towards me. It gave me a little comfort to know I wouldn't immediately feel groping hands on my frame. I laid down besides her, my back towards her own as I settled down, closing my eyes while simultaneously gripping the covers closer. I hoped maybe she would be too tired or too disinterested in me at the moment to try anything though something inside of me said otherwise. I tucked my head on the pillow, closing my eyes as I could sense the last candle being blown out as the world my eyelids hid somehow managed to get a shade darker.

Then came the soft sounds of her settling to sleep and I thought maybe, just maybe, tonight I could rest with ease. I tried to settle down, no matter what happened tonight I wouldn't be able to stop it whether she took an interest in me or not. Eventually, I felt the gentle hand of sleep caress my face and I went out just like the candle Lux had blown out.

I wasn't for sure when I woke up. It was dark though from what I could tell. The curtains might've been thick but I could usually see the slivers of dawn's rosy fingers peeking through. It seemed the lady of the night still wore her bear skin cloak though. What I was sure of was why I had woken up exactly. My heart clenched but I made no effort to let Lux know I was awake. From what she understood, I was still fast asleep and unaware of her touch.

It was surprisingly soft, the calloused fingers gently tracing the bones in the back of my neck. In soft, sweeping patterns the pads of her fingers followed in an almost innocent manner as if familiarizing herself with my body. Which I was sure she was doing just as I had figured it would happen. I laid still, figuring she might lose interest if she saw I didn't wake up to make a fuss but it didn't seem to be her goal to wake me up as she continued onwards.

Fingers slid from the back of my neck to around my waist gently, feeling and gliding along my sides for a moment before they settled around me. She was pressed her chest to my back, tucking my head under her chin and I wondered how long I could pretend to be asleep while she... She held me? I wasn't sure what to call it. I was sure she could feel hear loud my heart had gotten, feel the organ pulsing rapidly in the hollow chest cavity. She said nothing though if she knew. She just continued to hold me, I could feel her chin on the top of my head as she practically enveloped me in her grasp.

"You're awake, aren't you?" Her voice finally slipped past her lips, soft with the remains of slumber. She shifted slightly, she sounded half awake. "Don't lie, I know you are."

I paused, licking my lips for a moment. "I woke up a little bit ago." I said, deciding not to mention it was when she was touching my hair. I closed my eyes for a moment, fidgeting with the blanket in my grasp. The act of sleeping had coaxed me to bite down all my nervous habits but now that the illusion was broken? There was no point.

"I thought so but I figured you'd go back to bed."

I took a breath, slowly. "Is... Is there something you want from me? Tonight?" I finally gathered the courage to ask. There wasn't any need to agonize myself over tonight's events, waiting for them to unfold. It was best to get get it out of the way.

She paused, her breath hitched for a moment in her chest and I could feel it. She released it quickly enough though. "No. Not tonight. I don't feel like it."

I silently thanked whatever northern gods looked over this pack. Ukaya? It felt as if they would be the ones to watch over this. Though I wondered why she had reacted in such a way. Perhaps it was nerves,

Erisim had seemed to make himself clear that things had to proceed to how he had woven the threads of destiny.

"If that's what you wish." I told her quietly and closed my eyes, my heartbeat subdued for the moment as relief flooded me. "So you just want to sleep tonight?"

"I just want to sleep." She agreed, her grip around me readjusting. She seemed to settle down after reassuring me and it seemed herself of the fact.

"Goodnight Cyra."

"Goodnight Lux." I repeated quietly, laying there as I felt her slowly drift off. I stayed awake, unused to a touch that was so benevolent.

Chapter 22

My furs ended up never getting returned to me.

Weeks went by and the same routine persisted. Each night filled me with anxiety as I curled up under the fabrics of the bed yet each night nothing happened. I would ask softly and she would reply that she didn't feel like it and go back to nuzzling my hair or stroking the curve of my neck. If it wasn't so reassuring in the fact she wanted nothing from me, the anxiety would've killed me by now. I expected it every night and morning, in between the days when she'd see me and nothing came. It was as if she was on her best behavior.

Unfortunately, her brother was not. Samael had decided to make himself more known and I wasn't the only one who wasn't a fan of his. No one was it seemed. Lux kept him at a distance, the pack would draw themselves or children closer to them and watch stonily as he stalked through the halls. It seemed he had a reputation and I wondered if it had anything to do with what I had seen first hand.

The horror of the bloodstained clothes and the fate that seemed to have befallen my fellow Omegas. I hadn't seen them

I was in the nursery, it was where I preferred to spend my time at during the day. Anywhere else and I felt clumsy and awkward and it seemed none of the other girls who worked there minded me much either. In fact, the Delta's seemed to enjoy my help when it came to the little ones. The smaller pups too seemed to warm up to me as it became apparent that I was here to stay or maybe it was my slow but rapidly changing appearance. The dullness of my skin and eyes began to rapidly change into brighter features, my hair became sleeker and softer overall. I was beginning to change from the sickly thin Omega to someone who appeared to be a Delta if their nose was weak enough to mislead them. I felt better as well, less weak and even Lux seemed to notice the change. Her huge became stronger and she tried to occasionally take me out as if thinking I could handle the bitter cold better. Though the warmth of the nursery was what I mainly preferred to the cold.

I balanced a small pup in my arms, a chubby little girl who belonged to a Delta in the kitchen. Sometimes her mother would come with little pies for me whenever she came to pick up her baby. I smiled, brushing back her locks of pale gold. The baby giggled and I tickled her for a moment, laughing as well. Despite everything, each day it was beginning to become a little easier to laugh more freely. The first time I had done so in front of Lux I almost thought she might've had a stroke. Her face had frozen in place and her mouth agape, she looked so undignified and Alpha like I was sure something must've happened. In a flash, though the look had disappeared and she'd returned to her usual self. I settled the pup down after a moment, making sure to support her as she wobbly sat down. She'd just started to sit up and I was paranoid the poor thing would fall over and hurt herself somehow. The door opened with a click and I glanced up, surprised for a moment to see Lux. She never ventured into the nursery from what I knew.

"Cyra," She started to say as if she was almost surprised I was here. Her voice trailed but she only took another step into the warm, cozy little area. A few of the older children turned their heads, recognizing her. "I didn't know if you were here still or not. I came to come ask if you'd like to accompany me." She almost seemed to struggle to put the words together, her words lingering as if trying to find one another.

"Where to?" I asked. I'd grown more comfortable asking questions within the weeks. She hadn't done anything to once discourage me after all.

"Just somewhere."

She'd seemed a little annoyed for a moment when I asked so I didn't press further. Instead I stood and brushed my fingers through the babies hair once more before I glanced to the other nursery worker who seemed to acknowledge my leaving. "Alright, I'll come with you." I simply said as I followed her out into the halls.

She seemed to relax at that, happy that I had agreed to follow her which only made me wonder where she was taking me. I followed after her as she took the halls that seemed to lead back to he— our room. It was our room wasn't it? The thought suddenly struck me as we continued to walk. I almost thought about asking whether my furs would ever be returned but each time I braved to open my mouth, I couldn't bring myself to do it. I faltered in my courage. She opened our bedroom door and I stepped in, looking around as a bundle of nerves only grew in my stomach. Why was I here? I glanced towards her and she shut the door and promptly crossed her room to the door that was adjacent to the bathroom. I'd noticed it when I was first ushered in but had never thought to ask what lay behind it. It was a rather ornate piece of wood with carvings set into it and the handle being inlaid with crystals. She twisted it and opened it gently, glancing back to me as if to make sure I was coming along.

I peered into the room and followed after her quietly, the nerves growing. There wasn't any smell in the room to my knowledge and it was dark. If anyone had been inside, it hadn't been for a very long time. I could see faint shapes outlined but nothing more. Lux simply crossed over to a set of windows that were covered by heavy drapes before pulling them aside to reveal the rooms features. The discomfort in me only grew at what I saw.

"I had a dream last night, Ukaya visited me in it. They revealed to me something, a vision of the future. . . Our future." She said, gesturing to the room. "Tonight we start acting like proper mates, I've been childish and it ends tonight."

I didn't say anything, mutely still staring at what laid out before me. An old nursery, two cribs worn from age sat in front of me. The whole room reeked of dust as old toys laid strewn about and rugs stained from Gods only knew laid beneath our feet. The discomfort in my stomach only reached my throat as I realized the weight of her words and what they meant. Memories of such things flashing in my mind and my knees felt horribly weak.

"The nursery design is up to you, I expect you'll make it comfortable for the pups. You're allowed every resource for it and you can replace what you see fit even the cribs." She started to talk again, picking up a stuffed toy and wrinkling her nose at the dust that fell from it. "Especially the toys. . . All the important things that have value have been packed away and will be given later to them." She glanced towards me, pausing as she reached and gently touched my shoulder. "Of course, I'll gladly help in the process if you'd like me too. I'll be a good provider for you and a strong protector, everything you can wish for will be at your fingertips." She started to pull me close, wrapping me up in her arms. It took everything in me not to squirm.

"You'll see Cyra, things will be different after tonight."

Chapter 23

I loathed having to wait for night to fall after Lux's talk. She'd let me go, giving me a little journal of sorts and charcoal sticks to sketch and write out the things I would need for the nursery. Instead I had simply set the items down and mutely stared at them. The idea of somehow becoming pregnant with Lux's offspring set a wave of panic and sickness through me and so did the idea of planning the nursery. We weren't exactly a conventional couple in any means of the way. She hardly spoke to me and the times we did interact was during night when she'd ask me about my day or to simply pull me closer. It wasn't as if we were a couple of any sorts but rather two bodies that shared a room. I shuddered at the idea of things apparently changing as she promised. Changing into what? I glanced down towards the journal once more, unsure of what would even go into a nursery. Cribs yes but where would we get those? And to decorate it? I wouldn't know how or where to begin!

I curled my knees to my chest, nauseous as I continued to think about tonight. After Lux had left, I'd sat in the nursery on an old rocking chair, simply staring at the journal and charcoal sticks. The more that I looked at the old nursery, the more lost and trapped I seemed to feel. Homesickness struck me for a moment but not for my old pack but rather Calix. In all these weeks, his memory had floated from my mind but I never grabbed onto for long. What was he doing now? What was he thinking? Was he better off without me or was he worse? I knew I had certainly held him back from a lot of things but maybe he still fared the same. I was desperate for any familiar contact, someone to soothe my worries. Unsurprisingly, nothing and no one came though as I tucked my head between my knees and prayed for an answer, a deliverance of some sort.

Nothing came of that either. My Gods were a long ways away, by the eastern seas and in the timbered forests. They didn't reside in the ice and snow with these new Gods.

The hours trickled by, I didn't move from where Lux left me. Where would I go? I didn't feel confident enough to return to the nursery and act as if nothing had happened. I didn't want to wait in the bedroom for her to show. The dread of having to move only grew inside but was interrupted by the knock of a door. I paused, glancing over. It wasn't the nursery door but rather the bedroom. I got up, abandoning the notebook and sticks as I went to answer it. I knew it couldn't have been Lux and the thought was a soothing one. As I twisted the handle, I suddenly found myself face to face with Saskia. She smiled.

"Lux told me you'd still be in here, planning the nursery." She said with a little smile for a moment. "Are you excited? You always seem to do so well with the pups, including my little Tulip and the boys so I'm sure you must be excited at the possibility of your own little ones." She mused, her hands clasped together.

I didn't answer.

She seemed to understand that the subject was a sore one because she didn't broach it again. "Oh. . . Well, the mystic sent for you. She has things to discuss with you I imagine." She said, stepping back.

I nodded and she watched for a moment as she turned, leading me back from the room down and into the halls. I was beginning to feel as if the mystic was becoming annoyed with her retrieval of me. I could only hope it wouldn't be like last time in which she rubbed me down with strange oils and forced me to take baths. The idea was uncomfortable and as we stepped outside her hut, I found myself praying it wouldn't be anything like that. The door to the hut swung open and the sharp scent of herbs and oils struck me. The mystic looked impatient, waving me in but stopping Saskia once again. The Beta didn't seem to mind, only dipped her head in respect and turned away as the door shut.

"So it seems the day has finally come." The mystic started to speak, glancing back towards me as she reached and gently touched my cheek. "Maybe it's good we waited so long, you look healthier now." She mused quietly. "Night is almost on us and I need to get you ready. The Gods May bless you with a litter but they need the proper help to do so." She said as she started to open oils.

My nose wrinkled, I took a step back. "There must be some confusion, I'm an Omega, I'm barren." I stressed for a moment, discomfort evident in my voice. "I hardly even know Lux! We're not mates of any sort most certainly and I don't understand how I'm supposed to do anything you keep mentioning."

She glanced back towards me, clicking her tongue. "Sit down on the chair and I'll explain." She motioned me. I followed suit, hesitant but sitting down.

"Yes it is true you are an Omega and barren." She began to speak as she started to pour things into a bowl. Red powder and oils were sprinkled in and I could faintly smell the spiced aromas of whatever was being added. "But even your barrenness can be fixed with a Gods touch and Ukaya is sure to visit tonight after the ceremony." She said as she grabbed a pestle, grinding whatever was added into the bowl. "Their a fertility God and even though your pairing for better words lack the necessary parts, it's still possible for you to conceive a child with their help." She said, pausing to add something else. "Still, there is the matter of your relationship to Lux but even Ukaya can't help completely with that." She shook her head, setting the pestle down. I could faintly see a sort of paste clinging to the object.

I watched her grab a paintbrush. "Now strip, I need to start the preparations."

Chapter 24

I laid back on the bed, the feeling of sticky paint drying on my stomach prevalent. The mystic had spent a good chunk of time mixing the reddish colored paint onto my skin till it looked like I'd been mauled. The swirling symbols centered on my stomach and in strong lines wrapped around my inner thighs and down to my knees before coming back up to connect. I hadn't bothered to truly study the design, after she'd finished, she'd promptly kicked me out and told me to go lay down and wait for Lux to appear. So I had gone back and stripped, feeling cold and exposed as I waited for the Alpha to show. I could feel the tightness of my throat with every swallow I took. The anxiety of waiting for the Alpha to appear was growing in my gut, twisting them as I looked to my knees that were propped up. Faintly, I wondered if she would make it quick. I wasn't too sure how the evening was supposed to go, I'd never been with a female after all.

My head lolled back against the pillow, how long had it been? Perhaps Lux was busy and she'd forgotten? Maybe despite the threat of the Gods, she still refused? I could feel my heart fluttering hopefully almost at the idea. If I looked down to my chest, I could almost swear I saw the faint movement of the organ from underneath my skin as it pulsed. Still, I tried to calm myself. Even if she did show, it would be no different than the other times. Surely if I could survive that, I could survive this?

The door opened and I jumped, tensing for a moment as I sat up slightly to see the door had shut and Lux stood in front of it. I felt once again shamefully exposed in my lack of clothing. It was simply bare skin and paint for the other to see. The thrumming in my chest grew as I watched her simply take my form in. I couldn't tell if it was an appreciate gaze or not. Though I doubted it was anything positive. I simply shifted my gaze away after a moment as I felt the bed dip down besides me.

"Are you. . . Comfortable?" She asked, her voice had seemed to take on a thickness to it for a moment. "I want you to be comfortable." She said and the bed dipped further as she came to lean over me. "Would you prefer if I undressed myself?"

I paused, cheeks flushed for a moment as I couldn't help but find it embarrassing. I nodded slightly to her. I had no desire to undress her myself.

She nodded and sat back up and from the corner of my eye, I watched her shrug off her furs. Underneath the furs, I wasn't surprised to see hard sculpted muscles on the Alpha. Lux had always seemed to be so careful of undressing and being dressed properly before bed, I hadn't seen much of her besides her well sculpted arms but I had felt the power in them when she went to wrap me up. I was unsurprised to find the rest of her just as well toned and strong looking. A few odd scars littered her body, what appeared to be claw marks slashed up her abdomen in what appeared to have been a painful manner. The Alpha finished undressing till it was both of us on the bed, bare and waiting.

She cleared her throat again, leaning down for a moment as she gently touched the side of my face. Something she'd never done before as she brought me to look at her. "I'm supposed to kiss you." She hesitated, awkwardness showing in her. "Would. . . Would you sit up so I could?"

I pushed myself up for a moment but before I fully could, she had suddenly grabbed me and pulled me onto her lap. On instinct I gripped her shoulders, my cheeks flushed as I tried to ignore bare skin brushing against each other. She looked determined as ever, the same stoic look she had on most times overtaking her face as she brushed back my hair. I could feel her hands drifting from my hips up to my shoulders and chest, slow and almost reluctant as if she didn't know what to do. She furrowed her brows for a moment, her lips pursed as she studied me. "Are you going to kiss me back?" She asked.

I didn't know what to say in the moment, already unnerved by her behavior and the actions we were performing. I simply nodded my head again, "Yes." I murmured, my voice quiet.

She nodded, seeming pleased for a moment before she tilted her head. This time her eyes were closed and she was leaning in and I knew what she was doing. I let her come to me, feeling her press her lips against mine as she let out a soft grunt. Despite my initial lack of interest, I couldn't help but feel a spark go off in my chest as I gingerly moved my lips against hers. I could feel her arms come up around my neck, hands pressing into my hair as she kissed me back with ease. Being pressed so close to her, for a moment I was shocked to find her heart beating just as fast. Or was it mine? I couldn't tell and as soon as I felt like I was working my way into a rhythm of the kiss, she pulled away. Instead, I found my skin tingled as her mouth went to my neck instead. I could feel the pearly fangs she bore scraping against my skin as she nibbled, her mouth trailing lower and lower before finally coming to my breast.

A breath hitched in my throat as I felt her lips and tongue latch on, suckling as if she were a pup trying to feed. Ever so faintly I was aware of her hand trailing and skipping over my abdomen and stroking my thighs. An uncomfortable pressure began to grow in between them, something slick leaking from my sex. As soon as she felt the wetness her mouth trailed back up to capture my lips in a kiss as I felt her gently nudge my legs aside, hesitating once more as she seemed to stroke the folds before pressing a finger in. For a moment I stiffened once more, gently gripping onto her shoulders and she stopped, pulling her hand away. She pulled back completely, tense.

"Lay down." She ordered.

"What?"

Before I could protest or ask more, she gripped underneath my knees and jerked them, causing me to fall back. I landed against the bed with my head among the pillows with a small oof of protest. I pushed myself up slightly to see her hands still on my knees and keeping them pried apart as she lowered her head down between my thighs. I shifted, uncomfortable at how exposed I felt as suddenly a soft cool wind hit my center and I squirmed more, letting out a small whine despite everything. I realized after a few moments she was blowing on my center and I felt my heartbeat rise as I realized her mouthful of fangs were ever so close to my more delicate parts. Though before I could pull away or simply make a noise of protest I felt some hot, warm, and wet licking a stripe up me. I couldn't hold in the little gasp that left my lips.

"Stay still little one." Her voice murmured as her hands left my knees and came to spread me further apart at my lips, the thatch of red hair not causing her any issues as she once again blew on my center. A rush of tingles filled me as the wind seemed to hit something a little more sensitive this time. My heart sped up and once again I felt her mouth descend down upon me, this time focusing on that area of sensitivity. I couldn't help how my hands twisted into the bed sheets for a moment, tugging on them harshly as choked gasps and cries escaped my throat and a sudden pressure built inside me. She seemed to pay no mind and simply kept up with her activity, a hand once more trailing back and pushing its way inside my heat. Though this time there was no discomfort and I was in no position to refuse and a second finger joined the first soon enough. I writhed against the bed, feeling fit to cry as the pressure and the odd sensation taking over me. Tears did spring to my eyes and I moaned whorishly to my horror.

"Come on Cyra, just let go. Let me take care of you for the night." She pulled her face away, her chin covered in juices and her fingers continued to pump inside. It wasn't like the last time I'd been subjected to this, it felt oddly different. Almost loving in a strange way. "Come on little one, finish already." She rumbled softly.

I squirmed, whining and panting before I felt something simply give inside of me and my thighs trembled as my body seized up. Another choked cry left my throat and I suddenly felt myself go limp as she pulled away. Blearily, I could feel and see her crawling on top of me, pressing a kiss to my lips despite the fact I could still taste myself on her.

"You did so good tonight." She said softly, reaching up and brushing back the hair stuck to my cheek from the tears. "Such a good girl, pleasing yourself for your Alpha." Each word was broken apart by a kiss, I was too tired to protest but each kiss made me feel warmth inside. "Would you mind pleasing me one last time?"

I nodded, still trying to catch my breath. So far, she had been so gentle and it was odd. Despite my hatred of such an activity and my anxiety, she had given me a choice! When I was presented with it, I still decided to go along.

"Alright, just stay like that. I'm close enough, just focus on this." She said, having shifted to straddle my face as she spread her lips apart to present the fleshy pink center. She motioned to a small bud though at sat near the top.

I nodded tiredly once more as her thighs came around my ears and she settled on my face. I was far too tired to care about the fear of her suffocating me with the muscular limbs but she kept most of her weight off of me. I decided to follow her instructions, my tongue hesitant to what I was about to introduce it to but licked a stripe to earn a deep groan in reward and a hand digging into my hair. My tongue focused upward, quickly finding the little bud as I suckled and lapped at it. Surprisingly, the taste wasn't as bad as I feared and I focused as she began to rock her hips while huffing and whining. Suddenly she tugged on my hair sharply and her body spasmed as a sudden rush of liquid filled my open mouth. I whined softly for a moment before she rolled off, now trying to catch her breath.

"Oh. . ." She panted heavily, "We should do this much more often."